He was possessed.

He had raped and murdered a helpless creature and the town had put him on trial for his life, not believing his story (*as, however, they had hundreds of others*) that he couldn't have stopped himself. He had been "possessed."

But by what?

What was the dreadful power that gripped people haphazardly and at random, causing them to commit monstrous crimes and then returning them to a normal life?

He didn't know.

But, if he could escape the hangman, he was prepared to spend his life finding out.

Other books by the same author:

Short Stories:
ALTERNATING CURRENTS
THE CASE AGAINST TOMORROW
TOMORROW TIMES SEVEN
THE MAN WHO ATE THE WORLD
TURN LEFT AT THURSDAY
THE ABOMINABLE EARTHMAN

Novels
SLAVE SHIP
EDGE OF THE CITY
DRUNKARD'S WALK

In collaboration with C. M. Kornbluth
THE SPACE MERCHANTS
SEARCH THE SKY
GLADIATOR-AT-LAW
PRESIDENTIAL YEAR
WOLFBANE
THE WONDER EFFECT

In collaboration with Jack Williamson
THE REEFS OF SPACE
STARCHILD

Anthologies
The STAR series (#1 through #6)
STAR OF STARS

All published by Ballantine Books, Inc.
101 Fifth Avenue, New York, N.Y. 10003

A
PLAGUE
OF
PYTHONS

Frederik Pohl

BALLANTINE BOOKS   •   NEW YORK

Ballantine Books, Inc., 101 5th Avenue,
New York, N. Y. 10003

For
Lester del Rey
well and truly called
The Magnificent

I

"HEY, CHANDLER," said Larry Grantz, the jailer, "I can get fifty to one for a conviction. What d'you think?"

"Go to hell," said Chandler.

"Come on. Let me in on it. You got any surprises for the judge?"

Chandler didn't answer. He didn't even look at the jailer. A man who was on his way to hell didn't have to worry about what people thought of him.

"Now, look," said the jailer, "you could maybe use a friend or two before long. What do you say? Listen, I can get five for one if you're going to plead guilty. Are you?"

"Why should I? I'm innocent."

"Oh, yeah, all right, but if you plead guilty and throw yourself on the mercy of the court— No? The hell with you, then."

The jailer stood in the doorway, picking his nose and looking at Chandler with dislike. That was all right. Chandler was getting used to it.

It was hard to believe that this was the late 20th century . . . the third decade of the Atomic Age, the era of spaceflight. Of course, there hadn't been much of that lately. Chandler wondered what the Mars expedition must be thinking these days, waiting for the relief-and-rotation ship that must be a year or two overdue by now. Assuming they were still alive, of course. . . .

"You're gonna go in there in a minute, Chandler," said Grantz, "and then it's too late. Why don't you be a sport and let me know what's up?"

Chandler said, "I've got nothing to tell you. I'm innocent."

"You gonna plead that way?" pressed the jailer.

"I'm going to plead that way."

"Ah, cripes, they'll shoot you sure."

Chandler shook his head. Meaning: that's not up to me. Grantz stared at him irresolutely.

Chandler changed position gently, since he still hurt pretty badly. He wished he had a watch, although there was no particular reason for him to worry about the time any more.

Five years before, back in the old days before the demons came, when he was helping design telemetry equipment for the Ganymede probe, Chandler would not have believed his life would be at stake in a witchcraft trial. Not even that. He wasn't accused of being involved in witchcraft. He was about to go on trial for his life for the far more serious crime of *not* being involved in witchcraft.

It was hard to believe—but believe it or not, it was happening. It was happening to him.

It was happening right now.

Grantz cocked an ear to a voice from outside the door, nodded, ground out his cigarette under a heel and said, "All right, fink. Just remember when they're pulling the trigger on you, you could have had a friend on the firing squad." And he opened the door and marched Chandler out.

Because of the crowd that was attracted by the sensational nature of the charges against him, they held Chandler's trial in the all-purpose room of the high school. It smelled of leather and stale sweat.

There was a mob. There must have been three or four hundred people present. They all looked at him exactly as the jailer had.

Chandler walked up the three steps to the stage, with the jailer's hand on his elbow, and took his place at the defendant's table. His lawyer was there already.

The lawyer, who had been appointed by the court over his vigorous protests, looked at him without emotion. He was willing to do his job, but his job didn't require him to like his client. All he said was, "Stand up. The judge is coming in."

Chandler got to his feet and leaned on the table while the bailiff chanted his call and the chaplain read some verses from John. He did not listen. The Bible verses came too late to help him, and besides he ached.

When the police arrested him they had not been gentle. There were four of them. They were from the plant's own security force and carried no guns. They didn't need any; Chandler had put up no resistance after the first few moments—that is, he stopped fighting as soon as he could stop—but the police hadn't stopped. He remembered that very clearly. He remembered the nightstick across the side of his head that left his ear squashed and puffy, he remembered the kick in the gut that still made walking painful. He even remembered the pounding on his skull that had knocked him out.

The bruises along his rib cage and left arm, though, he did not remember getting. Obviously the police had been mad enough to keep right on subduing him after he was already unconscious.

Chandler did not blame them—exactly. He supposed he would have done the same thing.

The judge was having a long mumble with the court stenographer, apparently about something which had happened in the Union House the night before. Chandler knew Judge Ellithorp slightly. He did not expect to get a fair trial. The previous December the judge himself, while possessed, had smashed the transmitter of the town's radio station, which he owned, and set fire to the building it occupied. His son-in-law had been killed in the fire.

Since the judge had had his own taste of hell, he would not be kind to Chandler.

Laughing, the judge waved the reporter back to his seat and glanced around the courtroom. His gaze touched Chandler lightly, like the flick of the hanging strands of cord that precede a railroad tunnel. The touch carried the same warning. What lay ahead for Chandler was destruction.

"Read the charge," ordered Judge Ellithorp. He spoke very loudly. There were more than six hundred persons in the auditorium; the judge didn't want any of them to miss a word.

The bailiff ordered Chandler to stand and informed him that he was accused of having, on the seventeenth day of June last, committed on the person of Margaret Flershem, a minor, an act of rape—"Louder!" ordered the judge testily.

"Yes, Your Honor," said the bailiff, and inflated his chest. "An Act of Rape under Threat of Bodily Violence," he cried; "and Did Further Commit on the Person of Said Margaret Flershem an Act of Aggravated Assault—"

Chandler rubbed his aching side, looking at the ceiling. He remembered the look in Peggy Flershem's eyes as he forced himself on her. She was only sixteen years old, and at that time he hadn't even known her last name.

The bailiff boomed on: "—and Did Further Commit on that Same Seventeenth Day of June Last on the Person of Ingovar Porter an Act of Assault with Intent to Rape, the Foregoing Being a True Bill Handed Down by the Grand Jury of Marecel County in Extraordinary Session Assembled, the Eighteenth Day of June Last."

Judge Ellithorp looked satisfied as the bailiff sat down, quite winded. While the judge hunted through the papers on his desk the crowd in the auditorium stirred and murmured.

A child began to cry.

The judge stood up and pounded his gavel. "What is it? What's the matter with him? You, Dundon!" The court attendant the judge was looking at hurried over and spoke to the child's mother, then reported to the judge.

"I dunno, Your Honor. All he says is something scared him."

The judge was enraged. "Well, that's just fine! Now we have to take up the time of all these good people, probably for no reason, and hold up the business of this court, just because of a child. Bailiff! I want you to clear this courtroom of all children under—" he hesitated, calculating voting blocks in his head—"all children under the age of six. Dr. Palmer, are you there? Well, you better go ahead with the—prayer." The judge could not make himself say "the exorcism."

"I'm sorry, madam," he added to the mother of the crying two-year-old. "If you have someone to leave the child with, I'll instruct the attendants to save your place for you." She was also a voter.

Dr. Palmer rose, very grave, as he was embarrassed. He glared around the all-purpose room, defying anyone to smile, as he chanted: "Domina Pythonis, I command you, leave! Leave, Hel! Leave, Heloym! Leave, Sother and Thetragrammaton, leave, all unclean ones! I command you! In the name of God, in all of His manifestations!" He sat down again, still very grave. He knew that he did not make nearly as fine a showing as Father Lon, with his resonant *in nomina Jesu Christi et Sancti Ubaldi* and his censer, but the post of exorcist was filled in strict rotation, one month to a denomination, ever since the troubles started. Dr. Palmer was a Unitarian. Exorcisms had not been in the curriculum at the seminary and he had been forced to invent his own.

Chandler's lawyer tapped him on the shoulder. "Last chance to change your mind," he said.

"No. I'm not guilty, and that's the way I want to plead."

The lawyer shrugged and stood up, waiting for the judge to notice him.

Chandler, for the first time, allowed himself to meet the eyes of the crowd.

He studied the jury first. He knew some of them casually—it was not a big enough town to command a jury of total strangers for any defendant, and Chandler had lived there most of his life. He recognized Pop Matheson, old and very stiff, who ran the railroad station cigar stand. Two of the other men were familiar as faces passed in the street. The forewoman, though, was a stranger. She sat there very composed and frowning, and all he knew about her was that she wore funny hats. Yesterday's had been red roses when she was selected from the panel; today's was, of all things, a stuffed bird.

He did not think that any of them was possessed. He was not so sure of the audience.

He saw girls he had dated in high school, long before he met Margot; men he worked with at the plant. They all glanced at him, but he was not sure who was looking out through some of those familiar eyes. The visitors reliably watched all large gatherings, at least momentarily; it would be surprising if none of them were here.

"All right, how do you plead?" said Judge Ellithorp at last.

Chandler's lawyer straightened up. "Not guilty, Your Honor, by reason of temporary pandemic insanity."

The judge looked pleased. The crowd murmured, but they were pleased too. They had him dead to rights and it would have been a disappointment if Chandler had pleaded guilty. They wanted to see one of the vilest criminals in contemporary human society caught, exposed, convicted and punished; they did not want to miss a step of the process. Already in the playground behind the school three deputies from the sheriff's office were loading their rifles, while the school janitor chalked lines around the handball court to mark where the crowd witnessing the execution would be permitted to stand.

All this, as Chandler very reasonably told himself, was quite insane. There were satellites in orbit in the skies overhead! Every home in the town owned a television set, although to be sure they now did nothing but serve as receptacles for the holding of seashells and flowers . . . and hopes for a better world. This was the 20th century!

But they gave every sign of being about to kill him as dead as though it were the seventeenth. The prosecution made its case very quickly. Mrs. Porter testified that she worked at McKelvey Bros., the antibiotics plant, where the defendant also worked. Yes, that was him. She had been attracted by the noise from the culture room last—let's

see—"Was it the seventeenth day of June last?" prompt-
ed the prosecutor, and Chandler's attorney instinctively
gathered his muscles to rise, hesitated, glanced at his client
and shrugged. That was right, it was the seventeenth.
Incautiously she went right into the room. She should have
known better, she admitted. She should have called the
plant police right away, but, well, they hadn't had any
trouble at the plant, you know, and—well, she didn't. She
was a stupid woman, for all that she was rather good-
looking, and insatiably curious. She had seen Peggy Flershem on the floor. "She was all *blood*. And her clothes
were—And she was, I mean her—her body was—" With
relentless tact the prosecutor allowed her to stammer out
her observation that the girl had clearly been raped. And
she had seen Chandler laughing and breaking up the
place, throwing racks of cultures through the windows,
upsetting trays. Of course she had crossed herself and tried
a quick exorcism but there was no visible effect; then
Chandler had leaped at her. "He was *hateful!* He was just
foul!" But as he began to attack her the plant police came,
drawn by her screams.

Chandler's attorney did not question.

Peggy Flershem's deposition was introduced without ob-
jection from the defense. But she had little to say anyway,
having been dazed at first and unconscious later. The plant
police testified to having arrested Chandler; a doctor de-
scribed in chaste medical words the derangements Chandler had worked on Peggy Flershem's virgin anatomy.
There was no question from Chandler's lawyer—and, for
that matter, nothing to question. Chandler did not hope to
pretend that he had not ravished and nearly killed one girl,
then done his best to repeat the process on another. Sitting
there as the doctor testified, Chandler was able to tally
every break and bruise against the memory of what his
own body had done. He had been a spectator then, too,
as remote from the event as he was now; but that was
why they had him on trial. That was what they did not
believe.

At twelve-thirty the prosecution rested its case, Judge

Ellithorp looking very pleased. He recessed the court for one hour for lunch, and Larry Grantz took Chandler back to the detention cell in the basement of the school.

Two Swiss cheese sandwiches and a wax paper carton of chocolate milk were on the desk. They were Chandler's lunch. As they had been standing, the sandwiches were crusty and the milk luke-warm. He ate them anyway. He knew what the judge looked pleased about. At one-thirty Chandler's lawyer would put him on the stand, and no one would pay very much attention to what he had to say, and the jury would be out at most twenty minutes, and the verdict would be guilty. The judge was pleased because he would be able to pronounce sentence no later than four o'clock, no matter what.

They had formed the habit of holding the executions at sundown. As, at that time of year, sundown was after seven, it would all go very well—for everyone but Chandler.

II

LARRY GRANTZ looked in, eating a wedge of pie from the diner across the street. "You want anything else?" he demanded.

"Coffee."

"Ah, you won't have time to drink it." Grantz licked his fingers. "Of course, if you wasn't such a bastard about tipping me off—" He waited a moment and, when Chandler did not reply, closed the door.

Chandler looked out the window. It was a nice day. Far outside, above and away, a thin pale line of cloud stretched itself across the horizon. Contrail. Chandler watched it, listening, and caught the distant thundering mumble of a transsonic jet.

He wondered what sort of hand was at its controls.

Where they came from no one knew, where they were

going no one could tell. None had ever landed in this little part of the world in a long time. Not even at the Air Force base. Not anywhere, in the years since that day of disaster when the old world came to an end. Every once in a while one rasped across the sky, on what errands Chandler could not guess.

In any event he had more pressing problems.

The odd thing about his dilemma was not merely that he was innocent—in a way, that is—but that many who were guilty (in a way; as guilty as he himself, at any rate) were free and honored citizens. Chandler himself was a widower because his own wife had been murdered. He had seen the murderer leaving the scene of the crime, and the man he had seen was in the courtroom today, watching Chandler's own trial. Of the six hundred or so in the court, at least fifty were known to have taken part in one or more provable acts of murder, rape, arson, theft, sodomy, vandalism, assault and battery or a dozen other offenses indictable under the laws of the state.

Of course, that could be said of almost any community in the world in those years; Chandler's was not unique. What had put Chandler in the dock was not what his body had been seen to do, but the place in which it had been seen to do it.

For everybody knew that medicine and agriculture were never molested by the demons.

Chandler's own lawyer had pointed that out to him the day before the trial. "If it was anywhere but at the McKelvey plant, all right, but there's never been any trouble there. You know that. The trouble with you laymen is you think of lawyers in terms of Perry Mason, right? Rabbit out of the hat stuff. Well, I can't do that. I can only present your case, whatever it is, the best way possible. And the best thing I can do for your case right now is tell you you haven't got one." At that time the lawyer was still trying to be fair. He was even casting around for some thought he could use to convince himself that his client was innocent, though he had frankly admitted as soon as he introduced himself that he didn't have much hope there.

Chandler protested that he didn't have to commit rape. He'd been a widower for a year, but—

"Wait a minute," said the lawyer. "Listen. You can't make an ordinary claim of possession stick, but what about good old-fashioned insanity?" Chandler looked puzzled, so the lawyer explained. Wasn't it possible that Chandler was—consciously, subconsciously, unconsciously, call it what you will—trying to get revenge for what had happened to his own wife?

"No," said Chandler, "certainly not!" But then he had to stop and think. After all, he had never been possessed before; in fact, he had always retained a certain skepticism about "possession"—it seemed like such a convenient way for anyone to do any illicit thing he chose—until the moment when he looked up to see Peggy Flershem walking into the culture room with a tray of agar disks, and was astonished to find himself striking her with the wrench in his hand and ripping at her absurdly floral-printed slacks. Maybe his case was different. Maybe it wasn't the sort of possession that struck at random; maybe he was just off his rocker.

Margot, his wife, had been cut up cruelly. He had seen his friend, Jack Souther, leaving his home hurriedly as he approached; and although he had thought that the stains on his clothes looked queerly like blood, nothing in that prepared him for what he found in the rumpus room. It had taken him some time to identify the spread-out dissection on the floor with his wife Margot . . .

"No," he told his lawyer, "I was shaken up, of course. The worst time was the next night, when there was a knock on the door and I opened it and it was Jack. He'd come to apologize. I—well, I got over it. I tell you I was possessed, that's all."

"And I tell you that defense will put you right in front of a firing squad," said his lawyer. "And *that's* all."

Five or six others had been executed for hoaxing; Chandler was familiar with the ritual. He even understood it, in a way. The world had gone to pot in the previous two years. The real enemy was out of reach; when any citizen might run wild and, when caught, relapse into his own self, terrified and sick, there was a need to strike back. But the enemy was invisible. The hoaxers were only whipping boys—but they were the only targets vengeance had.

The real enemy had struck the entire world in a single night. One day the people of the world went about their business in the gloomy knowledge that they were likely to make mistakes but with, at least, the comfort that the mistakes would be their own. The next day had not such comfort. The next day anyone, anywhere, was likely to find himself seized, possessed, working evil or whimsy without ever having formed the intention to do so . . . and helplessly. Demons? Martians? No one knew whether the invaders of the soul were from another world or from some djinn's bottle. All they knew was that they were helpless against them.

Chandler stood up, kicked the balled-up wax paper from his sandwiches across the floor and swore violently.

He was beginning to wake from the shock that had gripped him. "Damn fool," he said to himself. He had no particular reason. Like the world, he needed a whipping boy too, if only himself. "Damn fool, you know they're going to shoot you!"

He stretched and twisted his body violently, alone in the middle of the room, in silence. He *had* to wake up. He *had* to start thinking. In a quarter of an hour or less the court would reconvene, and from then it was only a steady, quick slide to the grave.

It was better to do anything than to do nothing. He examined the windows of his improvised cell. They were above his head and barred; standing on the table, he could see feet walking outside, in the paved playyard of the school. He discarded the thought of escaping that way; there was no one to smuggle him a file, and there was no time. He studied the door to the hall. It was not impossible that when the guard opened it he could jump him, knock him out, run . . . run where? The room had been a storage place for athletic equipment at the end of a hall; the hall led only to the stairs and the stairs emerged into the courtroom. It was quite likely, he thought, that the hall had another flight of stairs somewhere farther along, or through another room. What had he spent his taxes on these years, if not for schools designed with more than one exit in case of fire? But as he had not thought to mark an escape route when he was brought in, it did him no good.

The guard, however, had a gun. Chandler lifted up an edge of the table and tried to shake one of the legs. They did not shake; that part of his taxes had been well enough spent, he thought wryly. The chair? Could he smash the chair to get a club, which would give him a weapon to get the guard's gun? . . .

Before he reached the chair the door opened and his lawyer came in.

"Sorry I'm late," he said briskly. "Well. As your attorney I have to tell you they've presented a damaging case. As I see it—"

"What case?" Chandler demanded. "I never denied the acts. What else did they prove?"

"Oh, God!" said his lawyer, not quite loudly enough to be insulting. "Do we have to go over that again? Your claim of possession would make a defense if it had happened anywhere else. We know that these cases exist, but we also know that they follow a pattern. Some areas seem to be immune—medical establishments, pharmaceutical plants among them. So they proved that all this happened in a pharmaceutical plant. I advise you to plead guilty."

Chandler sat down on the edge of the table, controlling himself very well, he thought. He only asked: "Would that do me any good at all?"

The lawyer reflected, gazing at the ceiling. ". . . No."

Chandler nodded. "So what else shall we talk about? Want to compare notes about where you were and I was the night the President went possessed?"

The lawyer was irritated. He kept his mouth shut for a moment until he thought he could keep from showing it. Outside a vendor was hawking amulets: "St. Ann beads!

Witch knots! Fresh garlic, local grown, best in town!" The lawyer shook his head.

"All right," he said, "it's your life. We'll do it your way. Anyway, time's up; Sergeant Grantz will be banging on the door any minute."

He zipped up his briefcase. Chandler did not move. "They don't give us much time anyway," the lawyer added, angry at Chandler and at hoaxers in general but not willing to say so. "Grantz is a stickler for promptness."

Chandler found a crumb of cheese by his hand and absently ate it. The lawyer watched him and glanced at his watch. "Oh, hell," he said, picked up his briefcase and kicked the base of the door. "Grantz! What's the matter with you? You asleep out there?"

Chandler was sworn, gave his name, admitted the truth of everything the previous witnesses had said. The faces were still aimed at him, every one. He could not read them at all any more, could not tell if they were friendly or hating, there were too many and they all had eyes. The jurors sat on their funeral-parlor chairs like cadavers, embalmed and propped, the dead witnessing a wake for the living. Only the forewoman in the funny hat showed signs of life, looking alertly at Chandler, at the judge, at the man next to her, around the auditorium. Maybe it was a good sign. At least she did not have the frozen-in-concrete, guilty-as-hell look of the others.

His attorney asked him the question he had been waiting for: "Tell us, in your own words, what happened." Chandler opened his mouth, and paused. Curiously, he had forgotten what he wanted to say. He had rehearsed this moment again and again; but all that came out was:

"I didn't do it. I mean, I did the acts, but I was possessed. That's all. Others have done worse, under the same circumstances, and been let off. Just as Fisher was acquitted for murdering the Learnards, as Draper got off after what he did to the Cline boy. As Jack Souther over there was let off after he murdered my own wife. They should be. They couldn't help themselves. Whatever this thing is that takes control, I know it can't be fought. My God, you can't even *try* to fight it!"

He was not getting through. The faces had not changed. The forewoman of the jury was now searching systematically through her pocketbook, taking each item out and examining it, putting it back and taking out another. But between times she looked at him and at least her expression wasn't hostile. He said, addressing her:

"That's all there is to it. It wasn't me running my body. It was someone else. I swear it before all of you, and before God."

The prosecutor did not bother to question him.

Chandler went back to his seat and sat down and watched the next twenty minutes go by in the wink of an eye, rapid, rapid; they were in a hurry to shoot him. He could hardly believe that Judge Ellithorp could speak so fast; the jurymen rose and filed out at a gallop, zip, whisk, and they were back again. Too fast! he cried silently, time had gone into high gear; but he knew that it was only his imagination. The twenty minutes had been a full twelve hundred seconds. And then time, as if to make amends, came to a stop, abrupt, brakes on. The judge asked the jury for their verdict and it was an eternity before the forewoman arose.

She was beginning to look rather disheveled. Beaming at Chandler—*surely* the woman was rather odd, it couldn't be just his imagination—she fumbled in her pocketbook for the slip of paper with the verdict. But she wore an expression of suppressed laughter.

"I *knew* I had it," she cried triumphantly and waved the slip above her head. "Now, let's see." She held it before her eyes and squinted. "Oh, yes. Judge, we the jury, and so forth and so on——"

She paused to wink at Judge Ellithorp. An uncertain worried murmur welled up in the auditorium. "All that junk, Judge," she explained, "anyway, we unanimously— but *unanimously,* love!—find this son of a bitch innocent. Why," she giggled, "we think he ought to get a medal, you know? I tell you what you do, love, you go right over and give him a big wet kiss and say you're sorry." She stood drunkenly swaying, laughing at the courtroom.

The murmuring became something more like a mass scream.

"Stop her, stop her!" bawled the judge, dropping his glasses. "Bailiff! Sergeant Grantz!"

"Oh, cool it," cried the woman in the floppy hat. "Hi, there! That you, love?" A man in the front row leaped to his feet and waved to her. The scream became a shout, a single word: *Possessed!*

"I tell you what," shrieked the woman, "let's all sing. *Everybody!* 'For he's a fairly good fellow, for he's a fairly good fellow—' Come on now, loves! All together, for His Honor—"

The bailiff, half a dozen policemen, the judge himself were scrambling toward her, but they were fighting a tide of terrified people, flowing away. Possessed she clearly was. And she was not alone. The man in the front row sang raucously along with her; then he flopped like a rag doll, and someone behind him leaped to his feet and carried along with the song without missing a beat, then another, another . . . it was like some distant sorcerer at a selector switch, turning first one on, then another. The noise was bedlam. As the police closed in on her the woman blew them kisses. They fell away, as from leprosy, then hurled themselves grimly back, like a lynch mob.

She was giggling as they fell on her.

From under their scrambling bodies her voice gasped, "Oh, now, not so rough! Say! Got a cigarette? I've been wanting—"

The voice choked and spluttered; and then it screamed. It was a sound of pure hysteria. The police separated themselves and helped her up, still screaming, eyes weeping with terror. "Oh!" she gasped. "Oh! I—I couldn't *stop!*"

Chandler stood up and took one step toward the door. So much confusion. Such utter disorganization. There was a chance—

He stopped and turned. They would catch him before he got outside the door. He made a decision, caught his lawyer by the arm, jerked at it until he got the man's attention. All of a sudden he felt alive again. There was hope! Tiny, insubstantial, but—"

"Listen," he said rapidly. "You, damn it! Listen to me. The jury acquitted me, right?"

The lawyer was startled. "Don't be ridiculous. It's a clear case of—"

"Be a lawyer, man! You live on technicalities, don't you? Make this one work for me!"

The attorney gave him a queer, thoughtful look, hesitated, shrugged and got to his feet. He had to shout to be heard. "Your Honor! I take it my client is free to go."

He made almost as much of a stir as the sobbing woman, but he outshouted the storm. "The jury's verdict is on record. Granted there was an *apparent* case of possession. Nevertheless—"

Judge Ellithorp yelled back: "No nonsense, you! Listen to me, young man—"

The lawyer snapped, "Permission to approach the bench."

"Granted."

Chandler sat unable to move, watching the brief, stormy conference. It was painful to be coming back to life. It was agony to hope. At least, he thought detachedly, his lawyer was fighting for him; the prosecutor's face was a thundercloud.

The lawyer came back, with the expression of a man who has won a victory he did not expect, and did not want. "Your last chance, Chandler. Change your plea to guilty."

"But—"

"Don't push your luck, boy! The judge has agreed to accept a plea. They'll throw you out of town, of course. But you'll be alive." Chandler hesitated. "Make up your mind! The best I can do otherwise is a mistrial, and that means you'll get convicted by another jury next week."

Chandler said, testing his luck: "You're sure they'll keep their end of the bargain?"

The lawyer shook his head, his expression that of a man who smells something unpleasant. "Your Honor! I ask you to discharge the jury. My client wishes to change his plea."

... In the school's chemistry lab, an hour later, Chandler discovered that the lawyer had left out one little detail. Outside there was a sound of motors idling, the police car that would dump him at the town's limits; inside was a thin, hollow hiss. It was the sound of a Bunsen burner, and in its blue flame a crudely shaped iron changed slowly from cherry to orange to glowing straw. It had the shape of a letter "H."

"H" for "hoaxer." The mark they were about to put on his forehead would be with him wherever he went and as long as he lived, which would probably not be long. "H" for "hoaxer," so that a glance would show that he had been convicted of the worst offense of all.

No one spoke to him as Larry Grantz took the iron out of the fire, but three husky policemen held his arms while he screamed.

III

THE PAIN was still burning when Chandler awoke the next day. He wished he had a bandage, but he didn't, and that was that.

He was in a freight car—had hopped it on the run at the yards, daring to sneak back into town long enough for that. He could not hope to hitchhike, with that mark on him. Anyway, hitchhiking was an invitation to trouble.

The railroads were safe—far safer than either cars or air transport, notoriously a lightning rod attracting possession. Chandler was surprised when the train came crashing to a stop, each freight car smashing against the couplings of the one ahead, the engine jolting forward and stopping again.

Then there was silence. It endured.

Chandler, who had been slowly waking after a night of very little sleep, sat up against the wall of the boxcar and wondered what was wrong.

It seemed remiss to start a day without signing the Cross or hearing a few exorcismal verses. It seemed to be mid-morning, time for work to be beginning at the plant. The lab men would be streaming in, their amulets examined at the door. The chaplains would be wandering about, ready to pray a possessing spirit out. Chandler, who kept an open mind, had considerable doubt of the effectiveness of all the amulets and spells—certainly they had not kept him from committing a brutal rape—but he felt uneasy without them. . . . The train was still not moving. In the silence he could hear the distant huffing of the engine.

He went to the door, supporting himself with one hand on the wooden wall, and looked out.

The tracks followed the roll of a river, their bed a few feet higher than an empty three-lane highway, which in turn was a dozen feet above the water. As he looked out the engine brayed twice. The train jolted, then stopped again.

Then there was a very long time when nothing happened at all.

From Chandler's car he could not see the engine. He was on the convex of the curve, and the other door of the car was sealed. He did not need to see it to know that something was wrong. There should have been a brakeman running with a flare to ward off other trains; but there was not. There should have been a station, or at least a water tank, to account for the stop in the first place. There was not. Something had gone wrong, and Chandler knew what it was. Not the details, but the central fact that lay behind this and behind almost everything that went wrong these days.

The engineer was possessed. It had to be that.

Yet it was odd, he thought, as odd as his own trouble. He had chosen this train with care. It contained eight refrigerator cars full of pharmaceuticals, and if anything was known about the laws governing possession, as his lawyer had told him, it was that such things were almost never interfered with.

Chandler jumped down to the roadbed, slipped on the crushed rock and almost fell. He had forgotten the wound on his forehead. He clutched the sill of the car door, where an ankh and fleur-de-lis had been chalked to ward off demons, until the sudden rush of blood subsided and the pain began to relent. After a moment he walked gingerly to the end of the car, slipped between the cars, dodged the couplers and climbed the ladder to its roof.

It was a warm, bright, silent day. Nothing moved. From his height he could see the Diesel at the front of the train and the caboose at its rear. No people. The train was halted a quarter-mile from where the tracks swooped across the river on a suspension bridge. Away from the river, the side of the tracks that had been hidden from him before, was an uneven rock cut and, above it, the slope of a mountain.

By looking carefully he could spot the signs of a number of homes within half a mile or so—the corner of a roof, a glassed-in porch built to command a river view, a twenty-foot television antenna poking through the trees. There was also the curve of a higher road along which the homes were strung.

Chandler took thought. He was alive and free, two gifts more gracious than he had had any right to expect. However, he would need food and he would need at least some sort of bandage for his forehead. He had a wool cap, stolen from the high school, which would hide the mark, though what it would do to the burn on his skin was something else again.

Chandler climbed down the ladder. With considerable pain he gentled the cap over the great raw "H" on his forehead and turned toward the mountain.

A voice from behind him said, "Hey. What's that you've got on your head?"

Chandler whirled, mad and scared. There was a man at

the open doorway of the next boxcar, kneeling and looking out at him. He was a small man, by no means young.
He wore a dirty Army officer's uniform blouse over chi-
nos. His face was dirty and unshaven, his eyes were
red-rimmed and puffy, but his expression was serenely
interested.

"Now, where the hell did you come from?" demanded
Chandler. "I didn't see you."

"Perhaps you didn't look," the man said cheerfully,
untangled his legs and slipped down to the crushed gravel
at the side of the roadbed. He caught Chandler's shoulder
to steady himself. From twenty inches away his breath was
enough to knock Chandler down.

But the man did not seem drunk. He didn't even seem
hung over, though he walked awkwardly, like a man who
is just on his feet after a long illness, or a toddling child.
"Excuse," he said, pushing past Chandler and walking a
step or two toward the head of the train, staring toward
the engine.

As Chandler watched, the little man lurched, recovered
himself and spun to face him. The change in him was
instant; one moment he was staring reflectively down
the track, unhurried and calm; the next he was in a
flap of consternation and terror. His eyes were wide with
fright. His lips worked convulsively.

Alarmed, Chandler snapped, "What's the matter with
you?"

"I—" The man swallowed, and stared about him. Then
his eyes returned to Chandler. He took a step, put out a
hand and said, "I—"

Then his expression changed again.

His hand dropped. In a tone of friendly curiosity he
said, "I asked you what you had on your head. Fall
against a hot stove?"

Chandler was now thoroughly jumpy. He didn't understand what was going on, but he understood that he didn't
like it. And he didn't like the subject of their conversation.
He snapped, "It's a brand. I got it for committing murder
and rape, all right?"

"Oh?" The man nodded reflectively.

"Yeah. I was possessed . . . but they didn't believe me. So they put this 'H' on me. It stands for 'hoaxer.' "

"Too bad." The man returned to Chandler and patted his shoulder. "Why didn't they believe you?"

"Because it happened in a pharmaceutical plant. I don't know how it is where you come from, buddy, but where I live—lived—that sort of thing didn't happen in that kind of place. Only it does now! Look at this train."

The man smiled brightly. "You think the train is possessed?"

"I think the engineer is."

The man nodded, and glanced impatiently toward the bridge again. "Would that be so bad?"

"Bad? Where've you been?"

The little man apologized, "I mean, do all the—what do you call them? Do all the cases of possession have to be *wicked?*"

Chandler took a deep breath. He couldn't believe the little man was for real. He could feel the short hairs at the back of his neck prickling erect. Something smelled wrong. *Nobody* asked questions like that. . . . He said weakly, "I never heard of any that weren't. Did you?"

"Yes, maybe I did," flared the man defensively. "Why not? Nothing is *evil*. It's all what you make of it . . . and I could imagine times when that sort of affair could be good. I can imagine it carrying you up to the stars! I can imagine it filling your brain with a mind grand enough to *crack* your own. I can—"

His voice tapered off as he noticed Chandler's popeyed stare.

"I was only saying maybe," he apologized, hesitated, seemed about to speak again . . . and then turned and started off toward the head of the train at a dead run.

Chandler stared after him.

He scratched the area of skin around the seared place on his forehead, then turned and began to climb the mountain.

Twenty yards uphill he stopped as though he had run into a brick wall.

He turned and looked down the tracks, but the man

was out of sight. Chandler stood staring down the empty line of crushed rock, not seeing it. There was a big question in his mind. He was wondering just who he had been talking to.

Or what.

By the time he reached the first shelving roadway he had put that particular puzzle away in the back of his mind. He knocked on the first door he came to, a great old three-storey house with well tended gardens.

Half a minute passed. There was no answer and no sound. The air smelled warmly of honeysuckle and mown grass, with wild onions chopped down by the blades of the mower. It was pleasant, or would have been in happier times. He knocked again, peremptorily, and the door was opened at once. Evidently someone had been right inside, listening.

A man stared at him. "Stranger, what do you want?" He was short, plump, with an extremely thick and unkempt beard. It did not appear to have been grown for its own sake, for where the facial hair could not be coaxed to grow his skin had the gross pits of old acne.

Chandler said glibly: "Good morning. I'm working my way east. I need something to eat, and I'm willing to work for it."

The man withdrew, leaving the upper half of the Dutch door open. As it looked in on only a vestibule it did not tell Chandler much. There was one curious thing—a lath and cardboard sign, shaped like an arc of a rainbow, lettered:

WELCOME TO ORPHALESE

He puzzled over it and dismissed it. The entrance room, apart from the sign, had a knickknack shelf of Japanese carved ivory and an old-fashioned umbrella rack, but that added nothing to his knowledge. He had already guessed that the owners of this home were well off. Also it had been recently painted; so they were not demoralized, as so much of the world had been demoralized, by the coming of the possessors. Even the elaborate sculpturing of its hedges had been maintained.

The man came back and with him was a girl of fifteen or so. She was tall, slim and rather homely, with a large jaw and an oval face. "Guy, he's not much to look at," she said to the pockmarked man. "Meggie, shall I let him in?" he asked. "Guy, you might as well," she shrugged, staring at Chandler with interest but not sympathy.

"Stranger, come along," said the man named Guy, and led him through a short hall into an enormous living room, a room two storeys high with a ten-foot fireplace.

Chandler's first thought was that he had stumbled in upon a wake. The room was neatly laid out in rows of folding chairs, more than half of them occupied. He entered from the side, but all the occupants of the chairs were looking toward him. He returned their stares; he had had a good deal of practice lately in looking back at staring faces, he reflected.

"Stranger, go in," said the man who had let him in, nudging him, "and meet the people of Orphalese."

Chandler hardly heard him. He had not expected anything like this. It was a meeting, a Daumier caricature of a Thursday Afternoon Literary Circle, old men with faces like moons, young women with faces like hags. They were strained, haggard and fearful, and a surprising number of them showed some sort of physical defect, a bandaged leg, an arm in a sling or merely the marks of pain on the features.

"Stranger, go in," repeated the man, and it was only then that Chandler noticed the man was holding a pistol, pointed at him.

IV

CHANDLER SAT in the rear of the room, watching. There must be thousands of little colonies like this, he reflected;

with the breakdown of long-distance communication the world had been atomized. There was a real fear, well justified, of living in large groups, for they too were lightning rods for possession. The world was stumbling along, but it was lame in all its members; a planetary lobotomy had stolen from it its wisdom and plan. If, he reflected dryly, it had ever had any.

But of course things were better in the old days. The world had seemed on the brink of blowing itself up, but at least it was by its own hand. Then came Christmas.

It had happened at Christmas, and the first sign was on nationwide television. The old President, balding, grave and plump, was making a special address to the nation, urging good will to men and, please, let's everyone remember to use artificial trees because of the fire danger in the event of H-bomb raids. In the middle of a sentence twenty million viewers had seen him stop, look dazedly around and say, in a breathless mumble, what sounded like: *"Disht dvornyet ilgt."* He had then picked up the Bible on the desk before him and thrown it at the camera.

The last the televiewers had seen was the fluttering pages of the Book, growing larger as it crashed against the lens, then a flicker and blinding shot of the studio lights as the cameraman jumped away and the instrument swiveled to stare mindlessly upward. Twenty minutes later the President was dead, as his Secretary of Health, Education and Welfare, hurrying with him back to the White House, calmly took a hand grenade from a Marine guard at the gate and blew the President's party to fragments.

For the President's seizure was only the first and most conspicuous. *"Disht dvornyet ilgt."* C.I.A. specialists were playing the tapes of the broadcast feverishly, electronically cleaning the mumble and stir from the studio away from the words to try to learn, first, the language and second what the devil it meant; but the President who ordered it was dead before the first reel spun, and his successor was not quite sworn in when it became his time to die. The ceremony was interrupted for an emergency call from the War Room, where a very nearly hysterical four-star general was trying to explain why he had ordered the immediate firing of every live missile in his command against Washington, D.C.

Over five hundred missiles were involved. In most of the sites the order was disobeyed, but in six of them, unfortunately, unquestioning discipline won out, thus ending not only the swearing in, the general's weeping explanation, the spinning of tapes, but also some two million lives in the District of Columbia, Maryland, Virginia and (through malfunctioning guidance relays on two missiles) Pennsylvania and Vermont. But it was only the beginning.

These were the first cases of possession seen by the world in some five hundred years, since the great casting out of devils of the Middle Ages. A thousand more occurred in the next few days, a hundred in the next hours. The timetable was made up out of scattered reports in the wireservice newsrooms, while they still had facilities for spot coverage in any part of the world. (That lasted almost a week.) They identified 237 cases of possession by noon of the next day. Disregarding the dubious items—the Yankee pitcher who leaped from the Manhattan bridge (he had Bright's disease), the warden of San Quentin who seated himself in the gas chamber and, literally, kicked the bucket (did he know the Grand Jury was subpoenaing his books?)—disregarding these, the chronology of major cases that evening was:

8:27 PM, E.S.T.: President has attack on television.

8:28 PM, E.S.T.: Prime Minister of England orders bombing raid against Israel, alleging secret plot (not yet carried out).

8:28 PM, E.S.T.: Captain of USN *Ethan Allen,* surfaced near Montauk Point, orders crash dive and course change, proceeding submerged at flank speed to New York Harbor.

9:10 PM, E.S.T.: Eastern Airlines four-engine jet makes wheels-up landing on roof of Pentagon, breaking some 1500 windows but causing no other major damage (except to the people aboard the jet); record of this incident fragmentary because entire site charred black in fusion attack two hours later.

9:23 PM, E.S.T.: Rosalie Pan, musical comedy star, jumps off stage, runs up center aisle and vanishes in cab, wearing beaded bra, G-string and $2500 headdress. Her movements are traced to Newark airport where she boards TWA jetliner, which is never seen again.

9:50 PM, E.S.T.: Entire S.A.C. fleet of 1200 jet bombers takes off for rendezvous over Newfoundland, where 72% are compelled to ditch as tankers fail to keep refueling rendezvous. (Orders committing the aircraft originate with S.A.C commander, found to be a suicide.)

10:14 PM, E.S.T.: Submarine fusion explosion destroys 40% of New York City. Analysis of fallout indicates U.S. Navy Polaris missiles were detonated underwater in bay; by elimination it is deduced that the submarine was the *Ethan Allen.*

10:50 PM, E.S.T.: President's party assassinated by Secretary of Health, Education and Welfare; Secretary then dies on bayonet of Marine guard who furnished the grenade.

10:55 PM, E.S.T.: Satellite stations observe great nuclear explosions in China and Tibet.

11:03 PM, E.S.T.: Heavily loaded munitions barges exploded near North Sea dikes of Holland; dikes breached, 1800 square miles of reclaimed land flooded out . . .

And so on. The incidents were countless. But before long, before even the C.I.A. had finished the first playthrough of the tapes, before their successors in the task identified *Disht dvornyet ilgt* as a Ukrainian dialect rendering of, My God, it works!—before all this, one fact was already apparent. There were many incidents scattered around the world, but not one of them took place in Russia itself.

Warsaw was ablaze, China pockmarked with blasts, East Berlin demolished along with its western sector, in eight rounds fired from a U.S. Army nuclear cannon. But the U.S.S.R. had not suffered at all, as far as could be told by the prying eyes in orbit; and that fact was reason enough for it to suffer very greatly very soon.

Within minutes of this discovery what remained of the military strength of the Western world was roaring through airless space toward the most likely targets of the East.

One unscathed missile base in Alaska completed a full shoot, seven missiles with fusion warheads. The three American bases that survived at all in the Mediterranean fired what they had. Even Britain, which had already watched the fire-tails of the American missiles departing on suicide missions, managed to resurrect its own two proto-type Blue Streaks from their racks, where they had mold-ered since the cancellation of the British missile program. One of these museum-pieces destroyed itself in launching, but the other chugged painfully across the sky, the tortoise following the flight of the hares. It arrived a full half-hour after the newer, hotter missiles. It might as well not have bothered. There was not much left to destroy.

It was fortunate for the Communists that most of the Western arsenal had already spent itself in suicide. What was left wiped out Moscow, Leningrad and nine other cities. It was even fortunate for the whole world, for this was the Apocalypse they had dreaded, every possible nu-clear weapon committed. But the circumstances were such—hasty orders, often at once recalled; confusion; panic—that most were unfused, many others merely tore great craters in the quickly healing surface of the sea. The fallout was murderous but spotty.

And the conventional forces invading Russia found nothing to fight. The Russians were as confused as they. There were not many survivors of the very top brass, and no one seemed to know just what had happened.

Was the Secretary of the C.P., U.S.S.R. behind that terrible brief agony? As he was dead before it was over, there was no way to tell. More than a quarter of a billion lives went into mushroom-shaped clouds, and nearly half of them were Russian, Latvian, Tatar and Kalmuck. The Peace Commission squabbled for a month, until the break-down of a communications cut them off from their governments and each other; and in that way, for a time, there was peace.

This was the sort of peace that was left, thought Chandler looking around at the queer faces and queerer surroundings, the peace of medieval baronies, cut off from the world, untouched where the rain of fallout had passed by but hardly civilized any more. Even his own home town, trying to take his life in a form of law, reduced at last to torture and exile to cast him out, was not the civilization he had grown up in but something new and ugly.

There was a great deal of talk he did not understand because he could not quite hear it, though they looked at him. Then Guy, with the gun, led him up to the front of the room. They had constructed an improvised platform out of plywood panels resting on squat, heavy boxes that looked like empty ammunition crates. On the dais was a dentist's chair, bolted to the plywood; and in the chair, strapped in, baby spotlights on steel-tube frames glaring on her, was a girl. She looked at Chandler with regretting eyes but did not speak.

"Stranger, get up there," said Guy, prodding him from behind, and Chandler took a plain wooden chair next to the girl.

"People of Orphalese," cried the teen-age cutie named Meggie, "we have two more brands to save from the imps!"

The men and women in the audience cackled or shrilled, "Save them. Save them!" They all had a look of invisible uniforms, Chandler saw, like baseball players in the lobby of a hotel or soldiers in a diner outside the gate of their post; they were all of a type. Their type was something strange. Some were tall, some short; there were old, fat, lean and young among them; but they all wore about them a look of glowing excitement, muted by an aura of suffering and pain. They wore, in a word, the look of bigots.

The bound girl was not one of them. She might have been twenty years old or as much as thirty. She might have been pretty. It was hard to tell; she wore no makeup, her hair strung raggedly to her neck, and her face was drawn into a tight, lean line. It was her eyes that were alive. She saw Chandler and she was sorry for him. And he saw, as he turned to look at her, that she was manacled to the dentist's chair.

"People of Orphalese," chanted Guy, standing behind Chandler with the muzzle of the gun against his neck, "the *meeting* of the Orphalese Self-Preservation *Society* will now come to *order.*" There was an approving, hungry murmur from the audience.

"Well, people of *Orphalese,*" Guy went on in his singsong, "the agenda for the *day* is first the salvation of we *Orphalese* on McGuire's *Mountain.*"

("All saved, all of us saved," rolled a murmur from the congregation.) A lean, red-headed man bounded to the platform and fussed with the stand of spotlights, turning one of them full on Chandler.

"People of Orphalese, as we are *saved,* do I have your consent to *pass on* and proceed to the next order of *business?*"

("Consent, consent, consent," rolled the echo.)

"And then the *second* item of business is to *welcome* and bring to grace these two newly *found* and adopted *souls.*"

The congregation shouted variously: "Bring them to grace! Save them from the imps! Keep Orphalese from the taint of the beast!"

Evidently Guy was satisfied. He nodded and became more chatty. "Okay, people of Orphalese, let's get down to it. We got two new ones, like I say. Their spirits have gone wandering on the wind, or anyway one of them has, and you all know the et cetera. They have committed a wrong unto others and therefore unto themselves. Herself, I mean. Course, the other one could have a flame spirit in him too." He stared severely at Chandler. "Boys, keep an eye on him, why don't you?" he said to two men in the front row, surrendering his gun. "Meggie, you tell about the female one."

The teen-aged girl stepped forward and said, in a conversational tone but with modest pride, "People of

Orph'lese, well, I was walking down the cut and I heard this car coming. Well, I was pretty surprised, you know. I had to figure what to do. You all know what the trouble is with cars."

"The imps!" cried a woman of forty with a face like a catfish.

The girl nodded. "Most prob'ly. Well, I—I mean, people of Orph'lese, well, I was by the switchback where we keep the chevvy-freeze hid, so I just waited till I saw it slowing down for the curve—me out of sight, you know—and I rolled the chevvy-freeze out nice and it caught the wheels. Right over!" she cried gleefully. "Off the shoulder, people of Orph'lese, and into the ditch and over, and I didn't give it a chance to burn. I cut the switch and I had her! I put a knife into her back, just a little, about a quarter of an inch, maybe. Her pain was the breakin' of the shell that enclosed her understanding, like it says. I figured she was all right then because she yelled but I brought her along that way. Then Guy took care of her until we got the synod. Oh," she remembered, "and her tongue staggered a little without purpose while he was putting it on, didn't it, Guy?" The bearded man nodded, grinning, and lifted up the girl's foot. Incredulously, Chandler saw that it was bound tight with a three-foot length of barbed wire, wound and twisted like a tourniquet, the blood black and congealed around it. He lifted his shocked eyes to meet the girl's. She only looked at him, with pity and understanding.

Guy patted the foot and let it go. "I didn't have any more C-clamps, people of Orphalese," he apologized, "but it looks all right at that. Well, let's see. We got to make up our minds about these two, I guess—no, wait!" He held up his hand as a murmur began. "First thing is, we ought to read a verse or two."

He opened a purple-bound volume at random, stared at a page for a moment, moving his lips, and then read:

"Some of you say, 'It is the north wind who has woven the clothes we wear.'

"And I say, Ay, it was the north wind, but shame was

his loom, and the softening of the sinews was his thread.

"And when his work was done he laughed in the forest."

Gently he closed the book, looking thoughtfully at the wall at the back of the room. He scratched his head. "Well, people of Orphalese," he said slowly, "they're laughing in the forest all right, I guarantee, but we've got one here that may be honest in the flesh, probably is, though she was a thief in the spirit. Right? Well, do we take her in or reject her, O people of Orphalese?"

The audience muttered to itself and then began to call out:

"Accept! Oh, bring in the brand! Accept and drive out the imp!"

"Fine," said the teen-ager, rubbing her hands and looking at the bearded man. "Guy, let her go." He began to release her from the chair. "You, girl stranger, what's your name?"

The girl said faintly, "Ellen Braisted."

" '*Meggie,* my name is Ellen Braisted,' " corrected the teen-ager. "Always say the name of the person you're talkin' to in Orph'lese, that way we know it's you talkin', not a flame spirit or wanderer. Okay, go sit down." Ellen limped wordlessly down into the audience. "Oh, and people of Orph'lese,' said Meggie, "the car's still there if we need it for anything. It didn't burn. Guy, you go on with this other fellow."

Guy stroked his beard and assessed Chandler, looking him over carefully. "Okay," he said. "People of Orphalese, the *third* order of business is to *welcome* or reject this *other* brand saved from the imps, as may be your *pleasure.*"

Chandler sat up straighter now that all of them were looking at him again; but it wasn't quite his turn, at that, because there was an interruption. Guy never finished. From the valley, far below, there was a sudden mighty thunder, rolling among the mountains. The windows blew in with a crystalline crash.

The room erupted into confusion, the audience leaping

from their seats, running to the broad windows, Guy and the teen-age girl seizing rifles, everyone in motion at once.

Chandler straightened, then sat down again. The red-headed man guarding him was looking away. It would be quite possible to grab his gun, run, get away from these maniacs. Yet he had nowhere to go. They might be crazy, but they seemed to have organization.

They seemed, in fact, to have worked out, on whatever crazed foundation of philosophy, some practical methods for coping with possession. He decided to stay, wait and see.

And at once he found himself leaping for the gun.

No. Chandler didn't find himself attacking the red-headed man. He found his *body* doing it; Chandler had nothing to do with it. It was the helpless compulsion he had felt before, that had nearly cost him his life; his body active and urgent and his mind completely cut off from it. He felt his own muscles move in ways he had not planned, observed himself leap forward, felt his own fist strike at the back of the red-headed man's ear. The man went spinning, the gun went flying, Chandler's body leaped after it, with Chandler a prisoner in his own brain, watching, horrified and helpless. And he had the gun!

He caught it in the hand that was his own hand, though someone else was moving it; he raised it and half-turned. He was suddenly conscious of a fusillade of gunfire from the roof, and a scattered echo of guns all round the outside of the house. Part of him was surprised, another alien part was not. He started to shoot the teen-aged girl in the back of the head, silently shouting, *No!*

His fingers never pulled the trigger.

He caught a second's glimpse of someone just beside him, whirled and saw the girl, Ellen Braisted, limping swiftly toward him with her barbed-wire amulet loose and catching at her feet. In her hands was an axe-handle club caught up from somewhere. She struck at Chandler's head, with a face like an eagle's, impersonal and determined. The blow caught him and dazed him, and from behind someone else struck him with something else. He went down.

He heard shouts and firing, but he was stunned. He felt himself dragged and dropped. He saw a cloudy, misty girl's face hanging over him; it receded and returned. Then a frightful blistering pain in his hand startled him back into full consciousness.

It was the girl, Ellen, still there, leaning over him and, oddly, weeping. And the pain in his hand was the burning flame of a kitchen match. Ellen was doing it, his wrist in one hand, a burning match held to it with the other.

V

CHANDLER YELLED hoarsely, jerking his hand away.

She dropped the match and jumped up, stepping on the flame and watching him. She had a butcher knife that had been caught between her elbow and her body while she burned him. Now she put her hand on the knife, waiting. "Does it hurt?" she demanded tautly.

Chandler howled, with incredulity and rage:

"God damn it, yes! What did you expect?"

"I expected it to hurt," she agreed. She watched him for a moment more and then, for the first time since he had seen her, she smiled. It was a small smile, but a beginning. A fusillade of shots from outside wiped it away at once. "Sorry," she said. "I had to do that. Please trust me."

"*Why* did you have to burn my hand?"

"House rules," she said. "Keeps the flame-spirits out, you know. They don't like pain." She took her hand off the knife warily. "It still hurts, doesn't it?"

"It still does, yes," nodded Chandler bitterly, and she lost interest in him and got up, looking about the room. Three of the Orphalese were dead, or seemed to be from the casual poses in which they lay draped across a chair on the floor. Some of the others might have been freshly wounded, though it was hard to tell the casualties from the others in view of the Orphalese custom of self-inflicted pain. There was still firing going on outside and overhead, and a shooting-gallery smell of burnt powder in the air. The girl, Ellen Braisted, limped back with the butcher knife held carelessly in one hand. She was followed by the teen-ager, who wore a smile of triumph—and, Chandler noticed for the first time, a sort of tourniquet of barbed-wire on her left forearm, the flesh puffy red around it. "Whopped 'em," she said with glee, and pointed a .22 rifle at Chandler.

Ellen Braisted said, "Oh, he—*Meggie*, I mean, he's all right." She pointed at his burned palm. Meg approached him with competent care, the rifle resting on her good right forearm and aimed at him as she examined his burn. She pursed her lips and looked at his face. "All right, Ellen, I guess he's clean. But you want to burn 'em deeper'n that. Never pays to go easy, just means we'll have to do something else to 'im tomorrow."

"The hell you will," thought Chandler, and all but said it; but reason stopped him. In Rome he would have to do Roman deeds. Besides, maybe their ideas worked. Besides, he had until tomorrow to make up his mind about what he wanted to do.

"Ellen, show him around," ordered the teen-ager. "I got no time myself. Shoosh! Almost got us that time, Ellen. Got to be more careful, 'cause the whitehanded aren't clean, you know." She strutted away, the rifle at trail. She seemed to be enjoying herself very much.

The name of the girl in the barbed-wire anklet was Ellen Braisted. She came from Lehigh County, Pennsylvania, and Chandler's first wonder was what she was doing nearly three thousand miles from home.

Nobody liked to travel much these days. One place was as bad as another, except that in the place where you were known you could perhaps count on friends and as a stranger you were probably fair game anywhere else.

Of course, there was one likely reason for travel. Chandler's own reason.

She didn't like to talk about it, that was clear, but that

was the reason. She had been possessed. When the teenager trapped her car the day before she had been the tool of another's will. She had had a dozen submachine guns in the trunk and she had meant to deliver them to a party of hunters in a valley just south of McGuire's Mountain. Chandler said, with some effort, "I must have been——"

"*Ellen,* I must have been," she corrected.

"Ellen, I must have been possessed too, just now. When I grabbed the gun."

"Of course. First time?"

He shook his head. For some reason the brand on his forehead began to throb.

"Well, then you know. Look out here, now."

They were at the great pier windows that looked out over the valley. Down below was the river, an arc of the railroad tracks, the wooded mountainside he had scaled. "Over there, Chandler." She was pointing to the railroad bridge.

Wispy gray smoke drifted off southward toward the stream. The freight train Chandler had ridden on had been stopped, all that time, in the middle of the bridge. The explosion that blew out their windows had occurred when another train plowed into it—evidently at high speed. It seemed that one of the trains had carried some sort of chemicals. The bridge was a twisted mess.

"A diversion, Chandler," said Ellen Braisted. "They wanted us looking that way. Then they attacked from up the mountain."

"Who?"

Ellen looked surprised. "The men that crashed the trains . . . if they *are* men. The ones who possessed me—and you—and the hunters. They don't like these Orphalese, I think. Maybe they're a little afraid of them. I think the Orphalese have a pretty good idea of how to fight them."

Chandler felt a sudden flash of sensation along his nerves. For a moment he thought he had been possessed again, and then he knew it for what it was. It was hope. "Ellen, I never thought of fighting them. I thought that was given up two years ago."

"So maybe you agree with me? Maybe you think it's worth while sticking with the Orphalese?"

Chandler allowed himself the contemplation of what hope meant. To find someone in this world who had a *plan!* Whatever the plan was. Even if it was a bad plan. He didn't think specifically of himself, or the brand on his forehead or the memory of the body of his wife. What he thought of was the prospect of thwarting—not even defeating, merely hampering or annoying was enough!—the imps, the "flame creatures," the pythons, devils, incubi or demons who had destroyed a world he had thought very fair.

"If they'll have me," he said, "I'll stick with them, all right. Where do I go to join?"

It was not hard to join at all.

Meg chattily informed him that he was already practically a member. "Chandler, we got to watch everybody strange, you know. See why, don't you? Might have a flame spirit in 'em, no fault of theirs, but look how they could mess us up. But now we know you don't, so—What do you mean, how do we know? Cause you *did* have one when you busted loose in there."

"I don't get it," said Chandler, lost. "You're saying that you know I don't have a, uh, flame spirit now because I did have one *then?*"

"Chandler, you'll catch on," said Meggie kindly, suppressing a smile. "Can't have two at a time, you see? So if you're the fella you are now, and the same fella you were *before,* you got to be honest-in-the-flesh yourself."

Chandler nodded thoughtfully. "Anyway, Chandler," the girl added, "we're going to take time off to eat now. You just make yourself at home. Soon's we start the synod up again we'll see 'bout letting you in."

Ellen Braisted asked, "Can I help with the food?" Meggie looked at her patiently and she corrected herself: "Meggie, can I help with the food?"

"Not this time, Ellen. Just stay out of the way a little." Ellen took Chandler's arm and led him to a sunporch.

All over the house the Orphalese were putting themselves back together again after the fight.

They didn't seem terribly upset, neither by their wounds nor their losses. They had, Chandler thought, a collective identity. The survival of the community was more important than any incidental damage to its members.

After three years of increasing alienation from a life he could not understand or accept, Chandler found that trait admirable. He liked their style. . . .

"Sorry about your hand," said Ellen Braisted.

He had not realized that he was rubbing it. "Oh, that's all right. I understand why you had to do it."

"Come over here." She opened a chest of first-aid supplies and took out cotton gauze. "Let me put this on it. You don't want it to stop hurting—that's the whole idea. But you don't want it getting infected. What's that business on your head?"

He touched the scar with his free hand. He had almost forgotten it.

He found it easy to tell her about it. When he was through she patted his arm. "Tough world. You say you were married?"

"Yes." He told her about Margot. And about Margot's death. She nodded, her face drawn.

"I was married too, Chandler," she said after a moment. "Lost my husband two years ago."

"Murdered?"

"Well," she said thoughtfully, "depends on what you mean by that. It was his own hand that did it. Got up one morning, went into the kitchen, came back looking like—I don't know—like his own evil nature. You know those cartoons? The Good You in white, the Bad You in black, whispering suggestions into your ear? He looked the Bad Him. And he cut his throat with a breadknife."

"Oh, God!" The words were jerked out of him. "Did he—didn't he say anything?"

"Yes, Chandler, he did. But I don't want to tell you what, because it was dirty and awful."

There was a smell of coffee percolating from inside the

house, and sounds of dishes and silverware. "Let's sit down over here," said Chandler, pointing to a chained swing that looked out over the darkening valley. "I guess your husband was possessed. Or as they say here, he had a flame spirit—"

"Ellen."

"Ellen, I mean," he corrected.

"Chandler," she said thoughtfully, "well, I don't quite go along with them on that. I've had quite a lot of experience with them, ever since my husband—ever since two years ago. They used me."

"For what?" Chandler demanded, startled. The concept of being *used* by the things was new, and peculiarly frightening. It was bad enough to view them as strange diabolic elements out of a hostile universe; to give them *purpose* was terrifying.

"You name it, Chandler," said the girl. "I did it. I've been practically all over the world in two years, because they used me for a messenger and—other things. They used me for all sorts of things, Chandler," she said very temperately, "and some of them I don't intend to discuss."

"Of course."

"Of course." Then she brightened. "But it wasn't all bad. You wouldn't believe some of the things—I flew a jet airplane to Lisbon once, Chandler! Would you believe it? And as a matter of fact, I don't even know how to drive a car very well. When I'm myself, I mean. I've been in Russia and England. I think I was in Africa once, although nobody ever mentioned the name and I wasn't sure. Just now, I came up from San Diego driving a great big truck, and— Well, it's been interesting. But I don't agree with the 'flame spirit' idea. They aren't ghosts or witches. They aren't creatures from outer space. Anyway, one of them is a man named Brad Fenell."

Chandler's heels dropped to the floor. The swing stopped with a clatter of its chains.

"A *man?*"

Ellen nodded soberly. "Or he was at one time, anyway," she corrected after a moment. "I used to go out with him when he lived next door to me in Catasauqua."

"But," cried Chandler, "what— How— How could he—"

She shook her head. "Now you're asking hard questions, Chandler. But I know this one—thing—was Brad Fenell. Brad asked me to marry him, and when I told him I wouldn't he—said those words I heard from my husband, just before he killed himself."

She stood up and turned toward the house. "And now," she said, "Meggie's calling us to eat. I hope I haven't spoiled your appetite."

All through the meal Chandler was preoccupied. He had to be spoken to twice before he responded, and then he had to be reminded to address the Orphalese by name.

He was trying to understand what Ellen had told him, and he was not succeeding. Real human beings? The monsters who had done such things?

It was, he thought somberly, more incredible to think of them as men than as demons from the pits of hell. . . .

The interrupted meeting was resumed after the place had been tidied up. The community had counted its losses and buried its dead.

There had been four of the attacking hunters. Even without their submachine guns, they had succeeded in killing eight Orphalese. But it was not all loss to the Orphalese, because two of the hunters were still alive, though wounded, and under the rules of this chessboard the captured enemy became a friend.

Guy had suffered a broken jaw in the scuffle and another man presided, a fat youth who favored a bandaged leg. He limped to his feet, grimacing and patting his leg. "O Orphalese and brothers," he said, "we have lost friends, but we have won a test. Praise the Prophet, we will be spared to win again, and to drive the imps of fire out of our world. Meggie, you going to tie these folks up?" The girl proudly ordered one of the hunters into the spotlighted dentist's chair, another into a wing chair that was hastily moved onto the platform. The men were bleeding and hurt, but they had clearly been abandoned by their possessors. They watched the Orphalese with puzzlement and fear.

"Walter, they're okay now," Meg reported as others finished tying up the hunters. "Oh, wait a minute." She advanced on Chandler. "Chandler, I'm sorry. You sit down there, hear?"

Chandler suffered himself to be bound to a camp chair on the platform and Walter took a drink of wine and opened the ornate book that was before him on the rostrum.

"Meg, thanks. Guy, I hope I do this as good as you do. Let me read you a little. Let's see." He put on his glasses and read:

" 'Much in you is still man, and much in you is not yet man, but a shapeless pigmy that walks asleep in the mist searching for its own awakening.' "

He closed the book, looked with satisfaction at Guy and said: "Do you understand that, new friends? They are the words of the Prophet, who men call Kahlil Gibran. For the benefit of the new folks I ought to say that he died this fleshly life quite a good number of years ago, but his vision was unclouded. Like we say, we are the sinews that batter the flame spirits but he is our soul." There was an antiphonal murmur from the audience and Walter flipped the pages again rapidly, obviously looking for a familiar passage. "People of Orphalese, here we are now. This's what he says. 'What is this that has torn our world apart?' The Prophet says: 'It is life in quest of life, in bodies that fear the grave.' Now, honestly, nothing could be clearer than that, people of Orphalese and friends! We got something taking possession of us, see? What is it? Well, he says here, People of Orphalese and friends, 'It is a flame spirit in you ever gathering more of itself.' Now, what the heck! Nobody can blame *us* for what a flame spirit *in* us does! So the first thing we got to learn, friends—and people of Orphalese—is, we aren't to blame. And the second thing is, we *are* to blame!"

He turned and grinned at Chandler kindly, while the chorus of responses came from the room. "Like here," he said, "people of Orphalese, the Prophet says *everybody* is guilty. 'The murdered is not unaccountable for his own murder, and the robbed is not blameless in being robbed. The righteous is not innocent of the deeds of the wicked, and the white-handed is not clean in the doings of the felon.' You see what he's getting at? We all got to take the responsibility for *everything*—and that means we got to suffer—but we don't have to worry about any special things we did when some flame spirit or wanderer, like, took us over.

"But we do have to suffer, people of Orphalese." His expression became grim. "Our beloved founder, Guy, who's sitting there doing a little extra suffering now, was favored enough to understand these things in the very beginning, when he himself was seized by these imps. And it is all in this book! Like it says, 'Your pain is self-chosen. It is the bitter potion by which the physician within you heals your sick self.' Ponder on that, people of Orphalese—and friends. No, I mean really ponder," he explained, glancing at the bound "friends" on the platform. "We always do that for a minute. Ada there will play us some music so we can ponder."

VI

CHANDLER SHIFTED uncomfortably, while an old woman crippled by arthritis began fumbling a tune out of an electric organ. The burn Ellen Braisted had given him was beginning to hurt badly. If only these people were not such obvious *nuts,* he thought, he would feel a lot better about casting his lot in with them. But maybe it took lunatics to do the job. Sane people hadn't accomplished much.

And anyway he had very little choice. . . .

"Ada, that's enough," ordered the fat youth. "Meg,

come on up here. People of Orphalese, now you can listen again while Meg explains to the new folks how all this got started, seeing Guy's in no condition to do it."

The teen-ager marched up to the platform and took the parade-rest position learned in some high school debating society—in the days when there were debating societies and high schools. "Ladies and gentlemen, well, let's start at the beginning. Guy tells this better'n I do, of course, but I guess I remember it all pretty well too. I ought to. I was in on it and all. I—" She grimaced and said, "Well, anyway, ladies and gentlemen—people of Orphalese—the way Guy organized this Orphalese self-protection society was, like Walter says, he was possessed. The only difference between Guy and you and me was that he knew what to do about it, because he read the book, you see. Not that that helped him at first, when he was took over. He was really seized. Yes, people of Orph'lese, he was taken and while his whole soul and brain and body was under the influence of some foul wanderer fiend from hell he did things that, ladies and gentlemen of Orph'lese, I wouldn't want to tell you. He was a harp in the hand of the mighty, as it says. Couldn't help it, not however much he tried. Only while he was doing—the things—he happened to catch his hand in a gas flame and, well you can see it was pretty bad." With a deprecatory smile Guy held up a twisted hand. "And, do you know, he was free of his imp right then and there! Now, Guy is a scientist, people of Orph'lese, he worked for the telephone company, and he not only had that training in the company school but he had read the book, you see, and he put two and two together. Oh, and he's my uncle, of course. I'm proud of him. I've always loved him, and even when he—when he was not one with himself, you know, when he was doing those terrible things to me, I knew it wasn't Uncle Guy that was doing them, but something else. I didn't know what, though. And when he told me he had figured out the Basic Rule, I went along with him every bit. I knew Guy wasn't wrong, and what he said was from Scripture. Imps fear pain! So we got to love it. That one I know by heart, all right: 'Could you keep your heart from wonder at the daily miracles of your life, your pain would not seem less wondrous than your joy.' That's what it says, right? So that's why we got to hurt ourselves, people of Orph'lese—and new brothers—because the wanderers don't like it when we hurt and they leave us alone. Simple's that.

"Well—" the girl's face stiffened momentarily—"I knew *I* wasn't going to be seized. So Guy and I got Else, that's the other girl he'd been doing things to, and we knew she wasn't going to be taken either. Not if the imps feared pain like Guy said, because," she said solemnly, "I want to tell you Guy hurt us pretty bad.

"And then we came out here, and found this place, and ever since then we've been adding brothers and sisters. It's been slow, of course, because not many people come this way any more, and we've had to kill a lot. Yes, we have. Sometimes the possessed just can't be saved, but—"

Abruptly her face changed.

Suddenly alert, her face years older, she glanced around the room. Then she relaxed . . .

And screamed.

Guy leaped up. Hoarsely, his voice almost inarticulate as he tried to talk with his broken jaw, he cried, "Wha . . . Wha's . . . *matter*, Meg?"

"Uncle Guy!" she wailed. She plunged off the platform and flung herself into his arms, crying hysterically.

"Wha?"

She sobbed, "I could feel it! They *took* me. Guy, you promised me they couldn't!"

He shook his head, dazed, staring at her as though she were indeed possessed—still possessed, and telling him some fearful great lie to destroy his hopes. He seemed unable to comprehend what she had said. One of the hunters bellowed in stark fear: "For God's sake, untie us! Give us a chance, anyway!" Chandler yelled agreement. In one split second everyone in the room had been transmuted by terror into something less than human. No one seemed capable of any action. Slowly the plump youth who had presided moved over to the hunter bound in the dentist's chair and began to fumble blindly at the knots.

Ellen Braisted dropped her head into her hands and began to shake.

The cruelty of the moment was that they had all tasted hope. Chandler writhed wildly against his ropes, his mind racing out of control. The world had become a hell for everyone, but a bearable hell until the promise of a chance to end it gave them a full sight of what their lives had been. Now that that was dashed they were far worse off than before.

Walter finished with the hunter and lethargically began to pick at Chandler's bonds. His face was slack and unseeing.

Then it, too, changed.

The plump youth stood up sharply, glanced about, and walked off the platform.

Ellen Braisted raised her face from her hands and, her eyes streaming, quietly stood up and followed. The old lady with the arthritis about-faced and limped with them. Chandler stared, puzzled, and then comprehended.

They were marching toward the corner of the room where the rifles were stacked. "Possessed!" Chandler bellowed, the words tasting of acid as they ripped out of his throat. "Stop them! You—Guy—look!" He flailed wildly at his loosened bonds, lunged, tottered and toppled, chair and all, crashingly off the platform.

The three possessed ones did not need to hurry; they had all the time in the world. They were already reaching out for the rifles when Chandler shouted. Economically they turned, raising the butts to their shoulders and began to fire at the Orphalese. It was a queerly frightening sight to see the arthritic organist, with a face like a relaxed executioner, take quick aim at Guy and, with a thirty-thirty shell, blow his throat out. Three shots, and the nearest three of the congregation were dead. Three more, and others went down, while the remainder turned and tried to run. It was like a slaughter of vermin. They never had a chance.

When every Orphalese except themselves was down on the floor, dead, wounded or, like Chandler, overlooked, the arthritic lady took careful aim at Ellen Braisted and the plump youth and shot them neatly in the temples. They didn't try to prevent her. With expressions that seemed almost impatient they presented their profiles to her aim.

Then the arthritic lady glanced leisurely about, fired into the stomach of a wounded man who was trying to rise, reloaded her rifle for insurance and began to search the bodies of the nearest dead. She was looking for matches. When she found them, she tugged weakly at the upholstery on a couch, swore and began methodically to rip and crumple pages out of Kahlil Gibran. When she had a heap of loose papers piled against the dais she pitched the remainder of the book out of the window, knelt and ignited the crumpled heap.

She stood watching the fire, her expression angry and impatient, tapping her foot.

The crumpled pages burned briskly. Before they died the wooden dais was beginning to catch. Laboriously the old lady toted folding chairs to pile on the blaze until it was roaring handsomely.

She watched it for several minutes, until it was a great orange pillar of fire sweeping to the ceiling, until the drapes on the wall behind were burning and the platform was a holocaust, until the noise of crackling flame and the beginning of plaster falling from the high ceiling proved that there was no likelihood of the fire going out and, indeed, no way to put it out without a complete fire department on the scene at once.

The old lady's expression cleared. She nodded to herself. She then put the muzzle of the rifle in her mouth and, with her thumb, pulled the trigger that blew the top of her head off. The body fell into the flames, but it was by then already dead.

Chandler had not been shot, but he was very near to roasting. Walter had released one hand and, while the possessed woman's attention was elsewhere, he had worked on the other knots.

When Chandler saw her commit suicide he redoubled

his efforts. It was incredible to him that his life had been saved, and he knew that if he escaped the flames he still had nothing to live for—that blasted brief hope had broken his spirit—but his fingers had a will of their own.

He lay there, struggling, while great black clouds of smoke, orange-painted from the flames, gathered under the high ceiling, while the thunder of falling lumps of plaster sounded like a child heaving volumes of the Encyclopedia Britannica down a flight of stairs, while the heat and shortage of oxygen made him breathe in violent spasms. Then he cried out sharply and stumbled to his feet. It was only a matter of moments before he was out of the house, but it was very nearly not time enough.

Behind him was a great, sustained crash. He thought it must have been the furniture on the upper floor toppling through the burned-out ceiling of the hall. He turned and looked.

It was dark, and now every window on the side of the house facing him was lighted. It was as though some mad householder had decided to equip his rooms only with orange lights that flickered and tossed. For a second Chandler thought there were still living people in the rooms—shapes moved and cavorted at the windows, as though they were gathering up possessions or waving wildly for help. But it was only the drapes, aflame, thrown about in the fierce heat.

Chandler sighed and turned away.

Pain was not a sure defense after all.

Evidently it was only an annoyance to the possessors . . . whoever, or whatever, they might be . . . as soon as they had become suspicious they had exerted themselves and destroyed the Orphalese. He listened and looked about, but no one else moved. He had not expected anyone. He had been sure that he was the only survivor.

He began to walk down the hill toward the wrecked railway bridge, turning only when a roar told him that the roof of the house had fallen in. A tulip of flame a hundred feet tall rose above the standing walls, and above that a shower of floating red-orange sparks, heat-borne, drifting up and away and beginning to settle all over the mountainside. Many were still red when they landed, a few still flaming. It was a distinct risk that the trees would begin to burn, and then he would be in fresh danger; but so great was his stupor that he did not even hurry.

By a plowed field he flung himself to the ground. He could go no farther because he had nowhere to go. He had had two homes and he had been driven from both of them; he had had hope twice, and twice he had been damned. He lay on his back, with the burning house mumbling and crackling in the distance, and stared up at the orange-lit tops of the trees and, past them, the stars. Over his left shoulder Deneb chased Vega across the sky; toward his feet something moved between the bright rosy dot that was Antares and another, the same brightness and hue—Mars? He spent several moments wondering if Mars were in that part of the heavens. Then he looked again for the tiny moving point that had crossed the claws of the Scorpion, but it was gone. A satellite, maybe. Although there were few of them left that the naked eye could hope to see. And there would never be any more, because the sort of accumulated wealth of nations that threw rockets into the sky was forever spent. It was probably an airplane, he thought drowsily, and drifted off to sleep without realizing how remote even that possibility had become. . . . He woke up to find that he was getting to his feet.

Once again an interloper tenanted his brain. He tried to interfere, although he knew how useless it was, but his own neck muscles turned his head from side to side, his own eyes looked this way and that, his own hand reached down for a dead branch that lay on the ground, then hesitated and withdrew. His body stood motionless for a second, the lips moving, the larynx mumbling to itself. He could almost hear words. Chandler felt like a fly in amber, imprisoned in his own brainbox. He was not surprised when his legs moved to carry him back toward the destroyed building, now a fakir's bed of white-hot coals with brush fires spattered around it. He thought he knew why. It seemed very likely that what possessor had him was a sort of clean-up squad, tidying up the loose ends of the slaughter; he expected that his body's errand was to destroy itself, and thus him, as all the others in the group of the Orphalese had been destroyed.

VII

CHANDLER'S BODY carried him rapidly toward the house. Now and then it paused and glanced about. It seemed to be weighing some shortcut in its errand; but always it resumed its climb.

Chandler could sympathize with it, in a way. He still felt every pain from burn, brand and wound; as they neared the embers of the building the heat it threw off intensified them all. He could not be a comfortable body to inhabit for long. He was almost sympathetic because his tenant could not find a convenient weapon with which to fulfill his purpose.

When it seemed they could get no closer without the skin of his face crackling and bursting into flame his body halted.

Chandler could feel his muscles gathering for what would be the final leap into the auto-da-fe. His feet took a short step—and slipped. His body stumbled and recovered itself; his mouth swore thickly in a language he did not know.

Then his body hesitated, glanced at the ground, paused again and bent down. It had tripped on a book. It picked the book up, and Chandler saw that it was the ripped Orphalese copy of Gibran's *The Prophet*.

Chandler's body stood poised for a moment, in an attitude of thought. Then it sat down, in the play of heat from the coals.

It was a moment before Chandler realized he was free. He tested his legs; they worked; he got up, turned and began to walk away.

He had traveled no more than a few yards when he stumbled slightly, as though shifting gears, and felt the tenant in his mind again.

He continued to walk away from the building, down toward the road. Once his arm raised the book he still carried and his eyes glanced down, as if for reassurance that it was the same book. That was the only clue he was given as to what had happened and it was not much. It was as though his occupying power, whatever it was, had gone—somewhere—to think things over, perhaps to ask a question of an unimaginable companion, and then returned with an altered purpose.

As time passed, Chandler began to receive additional clues, but he was in little shape to fit them together, for his body was near exhaustion. He walked to the road, and waited, rigid, until a pickup truck came bouncing along. He hailed it, his arms making a sign he did not understand, and when it stopped he addressed the driver in a language he did not speak. *"Shto,"* said the driver, a somber-faced Mexican in dungarees. *"Ja nie jestem Ruska. Czego pragniesh?"*

"Czy ty jedziesz to Los Angeles?" asked Chandler's mouth.

"Nyet. Acapulco."

Chandler's voice argued, *"Wes na* Los Angeles."

"Nyet." The voices droned on; Chandler lost interest in the argument and was only relieved when it seemed somehow to be settled and he was herded into the back of the truck. The somber Mexican locked him in; he felt the truck begin to move; his tenant left him, and he was at once asleep.

He woke long enough to find himself standing in the mist of early dawn at a crossroads. In a few minutes another car came by, and his voice talked earnestly with the driver for a moment. Chandler got in, was released, slept again and woke to find himself free and abandoned, sprawled across the back seat of the car, which was parked in front of a building marked Los Angeles International Airport.

Chandler got out of the car and strolled around, stretching. He realized he was very hungry.

No one was in sight. The field showed clear signs of having been through the same sort of destruction that had visited every major communications facility in the world. Part of the building before him was smashed flat and showed signs of having been burned; he saw projecting aluminum members, twisted and scorched but still visible aircraft parts; apparently a transport had crashed into the building. Burned-out cars littered the parking lot and what had once been a green lawn. They seemed to have been bulldozed out of the way, but not an inch farther than was necessary to clear the approach roads.

To his right, as he stared out onto the field, was a strange-looking construction on three legs, several storeys high. It did not seem to serve any useful purpose. Perhaps it had been a sort of luxury restaurant at one time, but now it too was burned out and glassless in its windows. The field itself was swept bare except for two or three parked planes in the bays, but he could see wrecked transports lining the approach strips. All in all, Los Angeles International Airport appeared to be serviceable, but only just.

He wondered where all the people were.

Distant truck noises answered part of the question. An Army six-by-six came bumping across a bridge that led from the takeoff strips to this parking area of the airport. Five men got out next to one of the ships. They glanced at him but did not speak as they began loading crates of some sort of goods from the truck into the aircraft, a four-engine, swept-wing jet of what looked to Chandler like an obsolete model. Perhaps it was one of the early Boeings. There hadn't been many of those in use at the time the troubles began, too big and fast for short hops, too slow to compete over long distances. But, of course, with all the destruction, and with no new aircraft being built anywhere in the world any more, no doubt they were as good as could be found.

The truckmen did not seem to be possessed; they worked with the normal amount of grunting and swearing, pausing to wipe sweat away or to scratch an itch. They showed neither the intense malevolent concentration nor the wide-eyed idiot curiosity of those whose bodies were no longer their own. Chandler settled the woolen cap over the brand on his forehead, to avoid unpleasantness, and drifted over toward them.

They stopped work and regarded him. One of them said something to another, who nodded and walked toward Chandler. "What do you want?" he demanded warily.

"I don't know. I was going to ask you the same question, I guess."

The man scowled. "Didn't your exec tell you what to do?"

"My what?"

The man paused, scratched and shook his head. "Well, stay away from us. This is an important shipment, see? I guess you're all right or you couldn't've got past the guards, but I don't want you messing us up. Got enough trouble already. I don't know why," he said in the tones of an old grievance, "we can't get the execs to let us *know* when they're going to bring somebody in. It wouldn't hurt them! Now here we got to load and fuel this ship and, for all I know, you've got half a ton of junk around somewhere that you're going to load onto it. How do I know how much fuel it'll take? No weather, naturally. So if there's headwinds it'll take full tanks, but it there's extra cargo I—"

"The only cargo I brought with me that I can think of is a book," said Chandler. "Weighs maybe a pound. You think I'm supposed to get on that plane?"

The man grunted non-committally.

"All right, suit yourself. Listen, is there any place I can get something to eat?"

The man considered. "Well, I guess we can spare you a sandwich. But you wait here. I'll bring it to you."

He went back to the truck. A moment later one of the others brought Chandler two cold hamburgers wrapped in wax paper, but would answer no questions.

Chandler ate every crumb, sought and found a washroom in the wrecked building, came out again and sat in the sun, watching the loading crew. He had become quite a fatalist. It did not seem that it was intended he should die immediately, so he might as well live.

There were large gaps in his understanding, but it seemed clear to Chandler that these men, though not possessed, were in some way working for the possessors. It was a distasteful concept; but on second thought it had reassuring elements. It was evidence that whatever the "execs" were, they were very possibly human beings—or, if not precisely human, at least they shared the human trait of working by some sort of organized effort toward some sort of a goal. It was the first non-random phenomenon he had seen in connection with the possessors, barring the short-term tactical matters of mass slaughter and destruction. It made him feel—what he tried at once to suppress, for he feared another destroying frustration—a touch of hope.

The men finished their work but did not leave. Nor did they approach Chandler, but sat in the shade of their truck, waiting for something. He drowsed and was awakened by a distant sputter of a single-engined Aerocoupe that hopped across the building behind him, turned sharply and came down with a brisk little run in the parking bay itself. From one side the pilot climbed down and from the other two men lifted, with great care, a wooden crate, small but apparently heavy. They stowed it in the jet while the pilot stood watching; then the pilot and one of the other men got into the crew compartment. Chandler could not be sure, but he had the impression that the truckman who entered the plane was no longer his own master. His movements seemed more sure and confident, but above all it was the mute, angry eyes with which his fellows regarded him that gave Chandler grounds for suspicion. He had no time to worry about that; for in the same breath he felt himself occupied once more.

He did not rise. His own voice said to him, "You. Votever you name, you fellow vit de book! You go get de book verever you pud it and get on dat ship dere, you see?" His eyes turned toward the waiting aircraft. "And don't forget de book!"

He was released. "I won't," he said automatically, and then realized that there was no longer anyone there to hear his answer.

Chandler retrieved the Gibran volume from where he had tossed it, turned and leaped out of the way. Another truck was racing toward them, gears racketing as the driver expertly down-shifted and brought it to a halt with a hiss of airbrakes. Chandler stared at the driver open-mouthed. The ten-wheeler was being driven by a girl of about fourteen.

She turned and shouted over her shoulder into the back of the truck, opened the door of the cab and jumped out. The side door of the truck swung open.

A girl of about eleven stood there. Behind her a young boy in a Scout uniform. They hopped to the ground and were followed by a dozen more, and another dozen, and more.

At least fifty children were piling out of that truck. Some were as young as ten, some as old as the girl driver. They were mixed boys and girls, about half and half. There were Japanese and Negroes, Mexicans and blue-eyed blonds. They formed into a ragged line and marched up the wheeled steps into the jet with a bird-twittering like the sound of a school bus on the way home.

Chandler followed them up the steps and turned to the loading crew standing by. They neither looked at him nor spoke. Inside the ship the children were larking and shouting about the rows of seats.

"What's going on?" Chandler asked.

"Shut up and get in." None of the men were looking at him. He couldn't even tell which one had spoken. All had the worried, angry, helpless expressions on their faces.

"Come on! Look, can't you at least tell me where we're going?"

"Get in." But one of them looked at him at last, for just a moment, then raised an arm and pointed.

He pointed west, out toward the Pacific, and to ten million square miles of nearly empty sea.

No lighted sign ordered fastening seat belts, no stewardess handed herself down the aisle between the seats to check on cigarettes. The loading crew slammed down the door from the outside, and shouted through it for Chandler to dog it down. Pilot and copilot were aboard already, but the door to their compartment was locked and Chandler never saw them. As he was levering down the latches that held the door the plane started its engines, blipped them once, wobbled over to a taxi strip . . . and took off. Just like that.

Chandler half fell into a seat and held on. The children shouted and sang, bouncing around the seats, pointing out the wrecked buildings of downtown Los Angeles as they slid by a few hundred feet under their wings. "Sit down!" Chandler shouted. "All of you! You'll get your necks broken—" But it was useless. They didn't refuse to obey him. They simply didn't hear. The take-off was quicker and more violent than any commercial flight. They rocketed up at full power (there would be no complaints about the noise from householders below), turned tightly in a bank that threw the children, laughing and shouting, into each other in heaps, and leveled off over the Pacific.

Chandler felt his ears popping. He got up, holding on to the back of the seat across the aisle. It had been a long time since he had been in an airplane. For a moment he thought he might be airsick, but the moment passed. The children had no such worries. They were acting like a class trip as the plane headed into the sun.

He counted and discovered there were fifty-two of the children. They were all around him, squeezing past in the aisle, calling to each other; but they didn't speak directly to him, nor he to them. They were in the coach section of the plane.

Chandler explored. The connecting door to the first class compartment was closed, but it was only fabric on a skeleton of metal rods. Chandler did not debate the advisability of breaking his way in; he just kicked it open and squeezed through, while the children watched him, and laughed and whispered to each other.

Most of the first class seats had been removed. A thin

scatter of crates and boxes were strapped to the floor. In the lounge section the divans were still in place, though, and Chandler cast himself down on one and closed his eyes.

He thought that it would be very easy to weep for Ellen Braisted. In a couple of hours she had come very close to him.

For that matter, he thought, turning his head to the back of the divan, the Orphalese were worth mourning too. Crazy, of course. A kinder term would be cultist. But out of their oddness had come an attempt to organize a life on a plan that *worked*.

Worked too well—for beyond doubt, the success of their defenses against the "flame spirits" was what had doomed them. The destruction of Orphalese was no lunatic caprice. It had been planned and methodically carried out, by a concerted effort involving at least a dozen—

At least a dozen what?

If Ellen Braisted were to be believed, human beings.

If a person wanted something to weep about, thought Chandler, the thought that it was human beings who had done all this was cause for tears enough. . . .

He slept. In spite of everything, he dropped off and did not wake for at least two or three hours, until the noise of the children woke him.

He stretched and sat up, feeling unutterably weary. Neither terror nor worry could stimulate him any more. He had reached that point of emotional exhaustion when the sudden thunder of shellfire or the unwarned banzai charge has lost its power to pump adrenalin into the blood; the glands were dry. He stared without emotion at the children standing before him.

"Mister!" cried one of them. "We're hungry."

He remembered having seen the boy before, getting out of the truck in his Boy Scout uniform, a child of about twelve, dark and dark-eyed.

"Yes," said Chandler, "I'm hungry too." He wished they were not there—wished they weren't on the plane at all; Chandler was not prepared to load his fragile confidence with the responsibility for fifty-two children, not when he could think of no way to take care even of himself. As a delaying tactic he asked, "Where'd all of you come from?"

But the boy would not be swerved. "St. Rose of Lima. That's a school out Venice way. Do you know if there's anything to eat?"

Chandler shook his head heavily. "I doubt it." He could not help trying to find something to discharge his responsibility, though; he added, "We ought to be landing pretty soon. Probably they'll feed you then."

The boy nodded, accepting the word of the adult. "Where we going, mister? China?"

Chandler almost laughed. But it might just *be* China, he thought; and admitted, "I'm not entirely sure. It might be Hawaii."

"Hawaii!" cried the teen-age girl behind him. "Keen! Say, there's surfing in Hawaii, right, mister?"

Chandler looked at her. Although he couldn't be sure, he thought she was the one who had been driving the truck and issuing the orders; but evidently the experience of being occupied had not left her with any extra information. He chose his words with care. "As a matter of fact, that's where surfing was invented, I think."

"Hey, that's great! But really," she added, "we're *awfully* hungry—"

Chandler roused himself. "Well, let's take a look," he said. He had no real hope of finding food, but anything was better than doing nothing while the children stood there looking at him. Just across the aisle was the flight kitchen.

It contained, as a matter of fact, a great deal of food.

Most of it was useless, in stacked trays in the warming ovens, so thoroughly decayed that it hardly even smelled any more. But there were also little packages of crackers, cheeses, jellies, macadamia nuts ... and cigarettes. Real cigarettes! Factory made!

Chandler put the Scout in charge of handing out the rations and, with trembling fingers, lit a cigarette. It was dried out with age, but it was delicious. Before he did anything else he filled his pockets with the little cardboard packs. Then he made himself some instant coffee with cold water, opened a can of the nuts and abandoned himself to his fate.

The children were far braver than he. At first Chandler thought it was merely the ignorance of youth. But he was wrong. They knew as much of what was ahead as he did—knew at least on what summons they were traveling, and how vile some of the creatures that summoned them could be; they had seen it happen in their own school. They almost reassured him with their careless pleasures in the food and the excitement of flying . . . until the hiss of the jets changed key, and Chandler realized his ears were popping again.

Outside the windows it was almost sunset again. Some of the children had been asleep in the reclining seats, others talking or playing with the empty cups and boxes of their feast. But they all waked and stared and commented. "It *is* Hawaii!" chortled the girl surfer. "Right, Mr. Chandler? I mean, look at those combers!"

"I think so—near as I can tell from the flying time." He raised his voice. "All of you! Sit down! Fasten the seat belts!" Surprisingly they obeyed.

The horizon dipped below the wingtip and straightened again, and there was a chorus of yells as they beheld land.

Chandler never saw the airfield. Only water; then beach; then water again, and some buildings. Then the plane staggered, slowed—trees appeared underneath them and to the sides—the wheels touched with a squeal and a jolt, and there was a roar of jets as the clamshells deflected their thrust forward to slow the plane down.

As the plane stopped, Chandler reached to unbuckle his seat belt—and found himself once more possessed.

His body strained to rise, surged against the belt and fell back. His lips exclaimed something irritable, in a language he did not understand; his hands went back to fumble with the buckle.

The girl surfer rose stiffly and said, "All right, children!

Stay together now. Come with me." She glanced incurious-
ly at Chandler and opened the door. The movable steps
were there already and the children filed out.

Chandler's body, mumbling to itself, got the belt open,
picked up the book and waited impatiently for the children
to get out of the way. Chandler was conscious of a horde
of men off to one side, pushing steps toward the other
door, but he could not turn his head to look.

As he descended the steps, out of the corner of his eye,
he saw the Boy Scout look toward him and wave, but
Chandler could not respond. Another swarm of men was
waiting for him to clear the steps. As soon as they could,
they hurried up and began stripping the aircraft of its
cargo.

He wondered at the rush but could not stop to watch
them; his legs carried him swiftly across a paved strip to
where a police car was cruising.

Chandler cringed inside, instinctively, but his body did
not falter as it stepped into the path of the car and raised
its hand.

The police car jammed on its brakes. The policeman at
the wheel, Chandler thought inside himself, looked startled,
but he also looked resigned. "To de South Gate, qvickly,"
said Chandler's lips, and he felt his legs carry him around
to the door on the other side.

There was another policeman on the seat next to the
driver. He leaped like a hare to get the door open and get
out before Chandler's body got there. He made it with
nothing to spare. "Jack, you go on, I'll tell Headquarters,"
he said hurriedly. The driver nodded without speaking. His
lips were white. He reached over Chandler to close the
door and made a sharp U-turn.

As soon as the car was moving Chandler felt himself
able to move his lips again.

"I—" he said. "I don't know—"

"Friend," said the policeman, "kindly keep your mouth
shut. 'South Gate,' the Exec said, and South Gate is where
I'm going."

Chandler shrugged and looked out the window . . . just

in time to see the jet that had brought him to the islands once more lumbering into life. It crept, wobbling its wing-tips, over the ground, picked up speed, roared across taxi strips and over rough ground and at last piled up against an ungainly looking foreign airplane, a Russian turbo prop by its markings, in a thunderous crash and ball of flame as its fuel exploded. No one got out.

It seemed that traffic to Hawaii was all one way.

VIII

THEY ROARED through downtown Honolulu with the siren blaring and cars scattering out of the way. At seventy miles an hour they raced down a road by the sea; Chandler caught a glimpse of a sign that said "Hilo," but where or what "Hilo" might be he had no idea. Soon there were fewer cars; then there were none but their own.

The road was a suburban highway lined with housing developments, shopping centers, palm groves and the occasional center of a small municipality, scattering helter-skelter together. There was a road like this extending in every direction from every city in the United States, Chandler thought; but this one was somewhat altered. Something had been there before them. About a mile outside Honolulu's outer fringe life was cut off as with a knife. There were no people on foot, and the only cars were rusted wrecks lining the roads. The lawns were ragged stands of weeds in front of the ranch-type homes.

It was evidently not allowed to live here.

Chandler craned his neck. His curiosity was becoming almost unbearable. He opened his mouth, but— "I said, 'Shut up,'" rumbled the cop without looking at him. There was a note in the policeman's voice that impressed Chandler. He did not quite know what it was, but it made him obey. They drove for another fifteen minutes in silence, then drew up before a barricade across the road.

Chandler got out. The policeman slammed the door behind him, ripping rubber off his tires with the speed of his U-turn and acceleration back toward Honolulu.

Chandler stood staring off after him, in bright warm sunlight with a reek of hibiscus and rotting palms in his nostrils. It was very quiet there, except for a soft scratchy sound of footsteps on gravel. As Chandler turned to face the man who was coming toward him, he realized he had learned one fact from the policeman after all. The cop was scared clear through.

Chandler said, "Hello," to the man who was approaching.

He too wore a uniform, but not that of the Honolulu city police. It was like U.S. Army suntans, but without insignia. Behind him were half a dozen others in the same dress, smoking, chatting, leaning against whatever was handy. The barricades themselves were impressively thorough. Barbed wire ran down the beach and out into the ocean; on the other side of the road, barbed wire ran clear out of sight along the middle of a side-road. The gate itself was bracketed with machine-gun emplacements.

The guard waited until he was close to Chandler before speaking. "What do you want?" he asked without greeting. Chandler shrugged. "All right, just wait here," said the guard, and began to walk away again.

"Wait a minute! What am I waiting for?" The guard shook his head without stopping or turning. He did not seem very interested, and he certainly was not helpful.

Chandler put down the fragmentary copy of *The Prophet* which he had carried so far and sat on the ground, but again he had no long time to wait. One of the guards came toward him, with the purposeful movements Chandler had learned to recognize. Without speaking the guard dug into a pocket. Chandler jumped up instinctively, but it was only a set of car keys.

As Chandler took them the look in the guard's eyes showed the quick release of tension that meant he was free again; and in that same moment Chandler's own body was occupied once more.

He reached down and picked up the tattered book.

Quickly, but a little clumsily, his fingers selected a key, and his legs carried him toward a little French car parked just the other side of the barrier.

Chandler was learning at last the skills of allowing his body to have its way. He couldn't help it in any event, so he was consciously disciplining himself to withdraw his attention from his muscles and senses. It involved queerly vertiginous problems. A hundred times a minute there was some unexpected body sway or movement of the hand, and his lagging, imprisoned mind would wrench at its unresponsive nerves to put out the elbow that would brace him, or to catch itself with a step. He had learned to ignore these things. The mind that inhabited his body had ways not his own of maintaining balance and reaching an objective, but they were equally sure.

He watched his own hands shifting the gears of the car. It was a make he had never driven, with a clutchless drive he did not understand, but the mind in his brain evidently understood it well enough. They picked up speed in great, gasoline-wasting surges.

Chandler began to form a picture of that mind. It belonged to an older man, from the hesitancy of its walk, and a testy one, from the heedless crash of the gears as it shifted. It drove with careless slapdash speed. Chandler's mind yelled and flinched in his brain as they rounded blind curves, where any casual other motorist would have been a catastrophe; but his hand on the wheel and his foot on the accelerator did not hesitate.

Beyond the South Gate the island of Oahu became abruptly wild.

There were beautiful homes, but there were also great, gap-toothed spaces where homes had once been and were no longer. It seemed that some monstrous Zoning Commissar had stalked through the island with an eraser, rubbing out the small homes, the cheap ones, the old ones; rubbing out the stores, rubbing out the factories. This whole section of the island had been turned into an exclusive residential park.

It was not uninhabited. Chandler thought he glimpsed a

few people, though since the direction of his eyes was not his to control it was hard to be sure. And then the Renault turned into a lane, paved but narrow. Hardwood trees with some sort of blossoms, Chandler could not tell what, overhung it on both sides.

It meandered for a mile or so, turned and opened into a great vacant parking lot. The Renault stopped with a squeal of brakes in front of a door that was flanked by bronze plaques:

TWA Flight Message Center.

Chandler caught sight of a skeletal towering form overhead, like radio transmitter antennae, as his body marched him inside, up a motionless escalator, along a hall and into a room.

His muscles relaxed.

He glanced around and, from a huge soft couch beside a desk, a huge soft body stirred and, gasping, sat up. It was a very fat old man, almost bald, wearing a coronet of silvery spikes.

He looked at Chandler without much interest. "Vot's your name?" he wheezed. He had a heavy, ineradicable accent, like a Hapsburg or a Russian diplomat. Chandler recognized it readily. He had heard it often enough, from his own lips.

The man's name was Koitska, he said in his accented wheeze. If he had another name he did not waste it on Chandler. He took as few words as possible to order Chandler to be seated and to be still.

Koitska squinted at the copy of Gibran's *The Prophet*. He did not glance at Chandler, but Chandler felt himself propelled out of his seat, to hand the book to Koitska, then returning. Koitska turned its pages with an expression of bored repugnance, like a man picking leeches off his arm. He seemed to be waiting for something.

A door closed on the floor below, and in a moment a girl came into the room.

She was tall, dark and not quite young. Chandler,

struck by her beauty, was sure that he had seen her, somewhere, but could not place her face. She wore a coronet like the fat man's, intertwined in a complicated hairdo, and she got right down to business. "Chandler, is it? All right, love, what we want to know is what this is all about." She indicated the book.

A relief that was like pain crossed Chandler's mind. So that was why he was here! Whoever these people were, however they managed to rule men's minds, they were not quite certain of their perfect power. To them the sad, futile Orphalese represented a sort of annoyance—not important enough to be a threat—but something which had proved inconvenient at one time and therefore needed investigating. As Chandler was the only survivor they had deemed it worth their godlike whiles to transport him four thousand miles so that he might bring them the book and satisfy their curiosity.

Chandler did not hesitate in telling them all about the people of Orphalese. There was nothing worth concealing, he was quite sure. No debts are owed to the dead; and the Orphalese had proved on their own heads, at the last, that their ritual of pain was only an annoyance to the possessors, not a tactic that could defeat them.

It took hardly five minutes to say everything that needed saying about Guy, Meggie and the other doomed and suffering inhabitants of the old house on the mountain.

Koitska hardly spoke. The girl was his interrogator, and sometimes translator as well, when his English was not sufficient to comprehend a point. With patient detachment she kept the story moving until Koitska with a bored shrug indicated he was through.

Then she smiled at Chandler and said, "Thanks, love. Haven't I seen you somewhere before?"

"I don't know. I thought the same thing about you."

"Oh, everybody's seen me. Lots of me. But—well, no matter. Good luck, love. Be nice to Koitska and perhaps he'll do as much for you." And she was gone.

Koitska lay unmoving on his couch for a few moments, rubbing a fat nose with a plump finger. "Hah," he said at last. Then, abruptly, "And now, de qvestion is, vot to do vit you, eh? I do not t'ink you can cook, eh?"

With unexpected clarity Chandler realized he was on trial for his life. "Cook? No, I'm afraid—I mean, I can boil eggs," he said. "Nothing fancy."

"Hah," grumbled Koitska. "Vel. Ve need a couple, three doctors, but I do not t'ink you vould do."

"You mean a medical doctor?" Chandler repeated stupidly.

"*Da, konyekhno.* Vot you t'ink I mean?" The fat man's voice was abruptly savage; it was very clear that to him Chandler was of far less importance than the bougainvillea that framed the parking lot outside.

Chandler said carefully, "I'm not a doctor, but I am an electrical engineer. Or was."

"Vas?"

"I haven't had much practice. There has not been a great deal of call for engineers, the last year or two."

"Hah." Koitska seemed to consider. "Vel," he said, "it could be . . . yes, it could be dat ve have a job for you. You go back downstairs and—no, vait." The fat man closed his eyes and Chandler felt himself seized and propelled down the stairs to what had once been a bay of a built-in garage. Now it was fitted up with workbenches and the gear of a radio ham's dreams.

Chandler walked woodenly to one of the benches. His own voice spoke to him, out of his own lips. "Ve got here someplace—*da,* here is cirguit diagrams an de specs for a sqvare-vave generator. You know vot dat is? Write down de answer." Chandler, released with a pencil in his hand and a pad before him, wrote *Yes.* "Okay. Den you build vun for me. I areddy got vun but I vant another. You do dis in de city, no here. Go to Tripler, dey tells you dere vere you can verk, vere to get parts, all dat. Couple days you come out here again, I see if I like how you build."

Clutching the thick sheaf of diagrams, Chandler felt himself propelled outside and back into the little car. The interview was over.

He wondered if he would be able to find his way back

to Honolulu, but that problem was then postponed as he discovered he could not start the car. His own hands had already done so, of course, but it had been so quick and sure that he had not paid attention; now he found that the ignition key was marked only in French, which he could not speak. After trial and error he discovered the combination that would start the engine and unlock the steering wheel, and then gingerly he toured the perimeter of the lot until he found an exit road.

It was close to midnight, he judged. Stars were shining overhead; there was a rising moon. He then remembered, somewhat tardily, that he should not be seeing stars. The lane he had come in on had been overhung on both sides with trees.

A few minutes later he realized he was quite lost.

Chandler stopped the car, swore feelingly, got out and looked around.

There was nothing much to see. The roads bore no markers that made sense to him. He shrugged and rummaged through the glove compartment on the chance of a map; there was none, but he did find a half-empty pack of cigarettes. He added them to the store in his pockets, lit up and relaxed.

Chandler felt exactly as he had felt the day he got his first job.

It was absolutely astonishing, he marveled at himself, but the mere suggestion of a possibility that there might somehow be some sort of an organized place for him in the lunatic framework of this world had calmed jumpy nerves he had almost forgotten he possessed. He puffed smoke over the top of the little car and admired the pleasant evening. There were the stars Vega and Deneb; it did not really seem to matter to him that the last time he had seen those stars, twenty-four hours before, he had just witnessed the murder of a score of innocents and considered his own life to be spent.

It would not be very hard to build a square-wave generator, if he could get parts. No doubt it was a sort of test. If he passed, he would get the job; and this Koitska would have little to worry about, too, because if anyone should somehow fake the test it would not take long to discover the deception, and Chandler had a good idea of what would happen to him or to anyone else whom Koitska caught in a deception—

He felt a light touch at his mind.

Or had he? He flicked the cigarette away, staring around. It was nothing, really. Or nothing that he could quite identify. It was as though he had been, well, nudged. It seemed that someone had paused on the threshold of usurping his body, but then unaccountably refrained.

As he had just about decided to forget it and get back into the car, he saw headlights approaching.

A low, lean sports car slowed as it came near, stopping beside him, and a girl leaned out, almost invisible in the darkness. "There you are, love," she said cheerfully. "Thought I spotted someone. Lost?"

She had a coronet, and Chandler recognized her. It was the girl who had interrogated him. "I guess I am," he admitted.

The girl leaned forward. "Come in, dear. Oh, that car? Leave it here, the silly little bug." She giggled as they drove away from the Renault. "Koitska wouldn't like you wandering around. I guess he decided to give you a job."

"How did you know?"

She said softly, "Well, love, you're still here, you know. What are you supposed to be doing?"

"Going to Tripler, whatever that is. In Honolulu, I guess. Then I have to build some radio equipment."

"Tripler's actually on the other side of the city. I'll take you to the gate; then you tell them where you want to go. They'll take care of it."

"I don't have any money for fare . . ."

She laughed at the idea. After a moment she said, "Koitska's not the worst. But I'd mind my step if I were you, love. Do what he says, the best you can. You never know. You might find yourself very fortunate . . ."

"I already think that. I'm alive."

"Why, love, that point of view will take you far."

She drove in silence for a minute. "Those Awful-Awfuls of yours—"

"The Orphalese?"

"Whatever you call them. They really didn't have much of a chance, you know." Chandler looked at her face, but it was shadowed. He wondered why she was taking the trouble to talk to him. Out of simple compassion? "Nobody does against the Exec," she said, her voice quite cheerful. "You get along best if you make up your mind to that right away."

The sports car slid smoothly to a stop at the barricade. In the floodlights above the machine-gun nests she looked more closely at Chandler. "What's that on your forehead, dear?"

Somehow he had lost the woolen cap, somewhere along the way. "A brand," he said shortly. " 'H' for hoaxer. I did something when one of you people had taken me over, and they thought I'd done it on my own."

The girl caught her breath, then laughed. "Why, this is wonderful!" she said excitedly. "No wonder I thought I'd seen you before. Don't you remember? I was the forewoman at your trial!"

IX

CHANDLER SPENT the night in a sort of hostel for casual employees of the Executive Committee. It had once been an Army hospital and was still run with the military's casual, loose-jointed efficiency. Everything he needed was provided for him—room, bedding, food, directions—but without anyone ever taking a moment to explain.

Still, the next morning, following the directions the desk orderly had given, Chandler boarded a pink and silver bus that took him to downtown Honolulu. The driver did not collect any fares. Chandler got off, as directed, at Fort

Street and walked a few blocks to the address he had been given. The name of the place was Parts 'n Plenty. He found it easily enough. It was a radio parts store; by the size of it, it had once been a big, well-stocked one; but now the counters were almost bare.

A thin-faced man with khaki-colored skin looked up and nodded. Chandler nodded back. He fingered a bin of tuning knobs, hefted a coil of two-strand antenna wire and said, "A fellow at Tripler told me to come here to pick up equipment, but I'm damned if I know what I'm supposed to do when I locate it. I don't have any money."

The dark-skinned man got up and came over to him. "Figured you for a malihini. No sweat. Have you got a list?"

"I can make one."

"All right. Catalogues on the table behind you, if you want them." He offered Chandler a cigarette and sat against the edge of the counter, reading over Chandler's shoulder. "Ho," he said suddenly. "Koitska's square-wave generator again, right?" Chandler admitted it, and the man grinned. "Every couple months he sends somebody along, Mr.—?"

"Chandler."

"Glad to know you. I'm John Hsi. Don't go easy on the job just because Koitska doesn't really need it, Chandler; it could be pretty important to you."

Chandler absorbed the information silently and handed over his list. The man did not look at it. "Come back in about an hour," he said.

"I won't have any money in an hour, either."

"Oh, that's all right. I'll put it on Koitska's bill."

Chandler said frankly, "Look, I don't know what's going on. Suppose I came in and picked up a thousand dollars worth of stuff, would you put that on the bill, too?"

"Certainly," said Hsi optimistically. "You thinking about stealing parts? What would you do with them?"

"Well . . ." Chandler puffed on his cigarette. "Well, I could—"

"No, you couldn't. Also, it wouldn't pay, believe me,"

Hsi said seriously. "If there is one thing that doesn't pay, it is cheating on the Exec."

"Now, that's another good question," said Chandler. "Who is the Exec?"

Hsi shook his head. "Sorry. I don't know you, Chandler."

"You mean you're afraid even to answer a question?"

"You're damned well told I am. Probably nobody would mind what I might tell you . . . but 'probably' isn't good enough."

Exasperated, Chandler said, "How the devil am I supposed to know what to do next? So I take all this junk back to my room at Tripler and solder up the generator—then what?"

"Then Koitska will get in touch with you," Hsi said, not unkindly. "Play it as it comes to you, Chandler, that's the best advice I can offer." He hesitated. "Koitska's not the worst of them," he said; and then, daringly, "and maybe he's not the best, either. Just do whatever he told you. Keep on doing it until he tells you to do something else. That's all. I mean, that's all the advice I can give you. Whether it's going to be enough to satisfy Koitska is something else again."

There is not much to do in a strange town when you have no money. Chandler's room at what once had been Tripler General Hospital was free; the bus was free; evidently all the radio parts he could want were also free. But he did not have the price of a cup of coffee or a haircut in the pockets of the suntan slacks the desk man at Tripler had issued him. He wandered around the streets of Honolulu, waiting for the hour to be up.

At Tripler a doctor had also examined his scar and it was now concealed under a neat white bandage; he had been fed; he had bathed; he had been given new clothes. Tripler was a teeming metropolis in itself, a main building some ten storeys high, a scattering of outbuildings connected to it by covered passages, with thousands of men and women busy about it. Chandler had spoken to a good many of them in the hour after waking up and before boarding the bus to Honolulu, and none of them had been free with information either.

Honolulu had not suffered greatly under the rule of the Exec. Remembering the shattered stateside cities, Chandler thought that this one had been incredibly fortunate. Dawdling down King Street, in the aromatic reek of the fish markets, Chandler could have thought himself in any port city before the grisly events of that Christmas when the planet went possessed. Crabs waved sluggishly at him from bins; great pinkscaled fish rested on nests of ice, waiting to be sold; smells of frying food came from half a dozen restaurants.

It was only the people who were different. There was a solid sprinkling of those who, like himself, were dressed in insignia-less former Army uniforms—obviously conscripts on Exec errands—and a surprising minority who, from overheard snatches of conversation, had come from countries other than the U.S.A. Russian mostly, Chandler guessed; but Russian or American, wearing suntans or aloha shirts, everyone he saw was marked by the visible signs of strain. There was no laughter.

Chandler saw a clock within the door of a restaurant; half an hour still to kill. He turned and wandered up, away from the water, toward the visible bulk of the hills; and in a moment he saw what made Honolulu's collective face wear its careworn frown.

It was an open square—perhaps it had once been a war memorial—and in the center of it was a fenced-off paved area where people seemed to be resting. It struck Chandler as curious that so many persons should have decided to take a nap on what surely was an uncomfortable bed of flat concrete; he approached and saw that they were not resting. Not only his eyes but his ears conveyed the message—and his nose, too, for the mild air was fetid with blood and rot.

These were not sleeping men and women. Some were dead; some were unconscious; all were maimed. The pavement was slimed with their blood. None had the strength to scream, but several were moaning and even some of the unconscious ones gasped like the breathing of a man in diabetic coma. Passersby walked briskly around the metal fence, and if their glances were curious it was at Chandler they looked, not at the tortured wrecks before them. He understood that the sight of the dying men and women was familiar—was painful—and thus was ignored; it was himself who was the curiosity, for staring at them. He turned and fled, trying not to vomit.

He was still shaken when he returned to Parts 'n Plenty. The hour was up but Hsi shook his head. "Not yet. You can sit down over there if you like." Chandler slumped into the indicated swivel chair and stared blankly at the wall.

The terror he had just seen was far worse than anything stateside; the random slaughter of murders and bombs was at least a momentary thing, and when it was done it was done; but this was sustained torture. He buried his head in his hands and did not look up until he heard the sound of a door opening.

Hsi, his face somehow different, was manipulating a lever on the outside of a door while a man inside, becoming visible as the door opened, was doing the same from inside.

It looked as though the lock on the door would not work unless both levers operated; and the man on the inside, whom Chandler had not seen before, was dressed, oddly, only in bathing trunks. His face wore the same expression as Hsi's.

Chandler guessed (with practice it was becoming easy!) that both were possessed. The man inside wheeled out two shopping carts loaded with electronic equipment of varying kinds, wordlessly received some empty ones from Hsi; and the door closed on him again.

Hsi tugged the lever down, turned, blinked and said, "All right, Chandler. Your stuff's here."

Chandler approached. "What was that all about?"

"Go to hell!" Hsi said with sudden violence. "I— Oh, never mind. Sorry. But I told you already, ask somebody else your questions, not me."

He gloomily began to pack the items on Chandler's list into a cardboard carton. Then he glanced at Chandler and said, half apologetically, "These are tough times, buddy. I guess there's no harm in answering *some* questions. You want to know why most of my stock's locked behind an armor-plate door? Well, you ought to be able to figure that out for yourself, anyway. The Exec doesn't like to have people playing with radios. Bert stays in the stockroom; I stay out here; twice a day the bosses open the door and we fill whatever orders they've approved. A little rough on Bert, of course—it's a ten-hour day in the stockroom for him, and nothing to do. But it could be worse. Oh, that's for sure, friend: It could be worse."

"Why the bathing suit? Hot in there?"

"Hot for Bert if they think he's smuggling stuff out," said Hsi. "You been here long enough to see the Monument yet?"

Chandler shook his head, then grimaced. "You mean up about three blocks that way? Where the people—?"

"That's right," said Hsi, "three blocks mauka from here, where the people— Where the people are serving as a very good object lesson to you and me. About a dozen there, right? Small for this time of year, Chandler. Usually there are more. Notice anything special about them?"

"They were butchered! Some of them looked like their legs had been burned right off. Their eyes gouged out, their faces—" Chandler brought up sharply. It had been bad enough looking at those wretched, writhing semi-cadavers; he did not want to talk about them.

The parts man nodded seriously. "Sometimes there are more, and sometimes they're worse hurt than that. Have you got any idea how they get that way? They do it to themselves, that's how. My own brother was out there for a week, last Statehood Day. He jumped feet first into a concrete mixer, and it took him seven days to die after I put him on my shoulder and carried him out there. I didn't like it, of course, but I didn't exactly have any choice; I wasn't running my own body at the time. Neither was he when he jumped. He was made to do it, because he used to have Bert's job and he thought he'd take a little short-wave set home. Like I said, you don't want to cheat on the Exec because it doesn't pay."

"But what am I supposed to——"

Hsi held up his hand. "Don't ask me how to keep out of that Monument bunch, Chandler. *I* don't know. Do what you're told and don't do anything you aren't told to do; that is the whole of the law. Now do me a favor and get out of here so I can pack up these other orders."

X

BY THE morning of the fourth day on the island of Oahu Chandler had learned enough of the ropes to have signed a money-chit at the Tripler currency office against Koitska's account. That was about all he had learned, except for a few practical matters like where meals were served and the location of the fresh-water swimming pool at the back of the grounds. He was killing time using the pool when, in the middle of a jackknife from the ten-foot board, he felt himself seized.

He sprawled into the water with a hard splashing slap, threshed about and, as he came to the surface, found himself giggling. "Sorry, dear," he apologized to himself, "but we don't carry our weight in the same places, you know. Get that square-what'sit thingamajig, like an angel, and meet me in front by the flagpole in twenty minutes."

He recognized the voice, even if his own vocal chords had made it. It was the girl who had driven him back from the interview with Koitska, the one who had casually announced she had saved his life at his hoaxing trial. Chandler swam to the side of the pool and toweled as he trotted toward his quarters. She was from Koitska now, of course; which meant that his "test" was about to be graded.

Quickly though he dressed, she was there before him,

standing beside a low-slung sports car and chatting with one of the groundskeepers. An armful of leis dangled beside her, and although she wore the coronet which was evidence of her status the gardener did not seem to fear her.

"Come along, love," she called to Chandler. "Koitska wants your thingummy. Chuck it in the trunk if it'll fit, and we'll head waikiki wikiwiki. Don't I say that nicely? But I only fool the malihinis, like you."

She chattered away as the little car dug its rear wheels into the drive and leaped around the green and out the gate.

The wind howled by them, the sun was bright, the sky was piercingly blue. Riding next to this beautiful girl, it was hard for Chandler to remember that she was one of those who had destroyed his world. It was a terrible thing to have so much hatred and to feel it so diluted.

Not even Koitska seemed a terrible enough enemy to accept such a load of detestation; it was hate without an object, and it recoiled on the hater, leaving him turgid and constrained. If he could not hate his onetime friend Jack Souther for defiling and destroying his wife, it was almost as hard to hate Souther's anonymous possessor.

It could have been Koitska. It could even have been this girl by his side. In the strange, cruel fantasies with which the Execs indulged themselves it was likely enough that they would sometimes assume the body, and the role, of the opposite sex. Why not? Strange, ruthless morality; it was impossible to evaluate it by any human standards.

It was also impossible to think of hatred with her beside him. They soared around Honolulu on a broad expressway and paralleled the beach toward Waikiki. "Look, dear. Diamond Head! Mustn't ignore it—very bad form—like not going to see the night-blooming cereus at the Punahou School. You haven't missed that, have you?"

"I'm afraid I have—"

"Rosalie. Call me Rosalie, dear."

"I'm afraid I have, Rosalie." For some reason the name sounded familiar.

"Shame, oh, shame! They say it was wonderful night before last. Looks like cactus to me, but—"

Chandler's mental processes had worked to a conclusion. "Rosalie *Pan!*" he said. "Now I know!"

"Know what? You mean—" she swerved around a motionless Buick, parked arrogantly five feet from the curb—"you mean you didn't know who I was? And to think I used to pay my press agent five thousand a year."

Chandler said, smiling, and almost relaxed, "I'm sorry, but musical comedies weren't my strong point. Let's see, wasn't there something about you disappearing—"

She nodded, glancing at him. "There sure was, dear. I almost froze to death getting out to that airport. Of course, it was worth it, I found out later. If I hadn't been took, as they say, I would've been dead. You remember what happened to New York about an hour later."

"You must have had some friends," Chandler began, and let it trail off.

So did the girl. After a moment she began to talk about the scenery again, pointing out the brick-red and purple bougainvillea, describing how the shoreline had looked before they'd "cleaned it up." "Oh, thousands and thousands of the *homeliest* little houses. You'd have hated it. So we have done at least a few good things, anyway," she said complacently, and began gently to probe into his life story. But as they stopped before the TWA Message Center, a few moments later, she said, "Well, love, it's been fun. Go on in; Koitska's expecting you. I'll see you later." And her eyes added gently: *I hope.*

Chandler got out of the car, turned . . . and felt himself taken. His voice said briskly, *"Zdrastvoi, Rosie. Gd'yeh Koitska?"*

Unsurprised the girl pointed to the building. *"Kto govorit?"*

Chandler's voice answered in English, with a faint Oxford accent: "It is I, Rosie, Kalman. Where's Koitska's tinkertoy? Oh, all right, thanks; I'll just pick it up and take it in. Hope it's all right. I must say one wearies of breaking in these new fellows."

Chandler's body ambled around to the trunk of the car, took out the square-wave generator on its breadboard base and slouched into the building. It called ahead in the same language and was answered wheezily from above: Koitska. *"Zdrastvoi. Kto, Kalman? Iditye suda ko mneh."*

"Konyekhno!" cried Chandler's voice and he was, carried in and up to where the fat man lounged in a leather-upholstered wheelchair. There was a conversation, long minutes of it, while the two men poked at the generator. Chandler did not understand a word until he spoke to himself: "You—what's your name."

"Chandler," Koitska filled in for him.

"You, Chandler. D'you know anything at all about submillimeter microwaves? Tell Koitska." Briefly Chandler felt himself free—long enough to nod; then he was possessed again, and Koitska repeated the nod. "Good, then. Tell Koitska what experience you've had."

Again free, Chandler said, "Not a great deal of actual experience. I worked with a group at Cal Tech on spectroscopic measurements in the million megacycle range. I didn't design any of the equipment, though I helped put it together." He recited his degrees until Koitska raised a languid hand.

"Shto, I don't care. If ve gave you diagrams you could build?"

"Certainly, if I had the equipment. I suppose I'd need—"

But Koitska stopped him again. "I know vot you need," he said damply. "Enough. Ve see." In a moment Chandler was taken again, and his voice and Koitska's debated the matter for a while, until Koitska shrugged, turned his head and seemed to go to sleep.

Chandler marched himself out of the room and out into the driveway before his voice said to him: "You've secured a position, then. Go back to Tripler until we send for you. It'll be a few days, I expect."

And Chandler was free again.

He was also alone. The girl in the Porsche was gone. The door to the TWA building had latched itself behind him. He stared around him, swore, shrugged and circled the building to the parking lot at back on the chance that a car might be there for him to borrow.

Luckily there was—there were four, in fact, all with keys in them. He selected a Ford, puzzled out the likeliest road back to Honolulu and turned the key in the starter.

It was fortunate, he thought, that there had been several cars; if there had been only one he would not have dared to take it, for fear of stranding Koitska or some other Exec who might easily blot him out in annoyance. He did not wish to join the wretches at the Monument.

It was astonishing how readily fear had become a part of his life.

The trouble with this position he had somehow secured—one of the troubles—was that there was no union delegate to settle employee grievances. Like no transportation. Like no clear idea of working hours, or duties. Like no mention at all—of course—of wages. Chandler had no idea what his rights were, if any at all, or of what the penalties would be if he overstepped them.

The maimed victims at the Monument supplied a clue, of course. He could not really believe that that sort of punishment would be applied for minor infractions. Death was so much less trouble. Even death was not really likely, he thought, for a simple lapse.

He *thought.*

He could not be sure, of course. He could be sure of only one thing: He was now a slave, completely a slave, a slave until the day he died. Back on the mainland there was the statistical likelihood of occasional slavery-by-possession, yet; but there it was only the body that was enslaved, and only for moments. Here, in the shadow of the Execs, it was all of him, forever, until death or a miracle turned him loose.

On the second day following, he returned to his room at Tripler after breakfast, and found a Honolulu city policeman sitting hollow-eyed on the edge of his bed. The man stood up as Chandler came in. "So," he grumbled, "you take so long! Here. Is diagrams, specs, parts lists, all. You get everything three days from now, then we begin."

The policeman, no longer Koitska, shook himself, glanced stolidly at Chandler and walked out, leaving a thick manila envelope on the pillow. On it was written, in a crabbed hand: *All secret! Do not show diagrams!*

Chandler opened the envelope and spilled its contents on the bed.

An hour later he realized that sixty minutes had passed in which he had not been afraid. It was good to be working again, he thought, and then that thought faded away again as he returned to studying the sheaves of circuit diagrams and closely typed pages of specifications.

It was not only work, it was hard work, and absorbing. Chandler knew enough about the very short wavelength radio spectrum to know that the device he was supposed to build was no proficiency test; this was for real. The more he puzzled over it the less he could understand of its purpose. There was a transmitter and there was a receiver. Astonishingly, neither was directional: that ruled out radar, for example. He rejected immediately the thought that the radiation was for spectrum analysis, as in the Cal Tech project—unfortunate, because that was the only application with which he had first-hand familiarity; but impossible. The thing was too complicated. Nor could it be a simple message transmitter—no, perhaps it could, assuming there was a reason for using the submillimeter bands instead of the conventional, far simpler shortwave spectrum. Could it? The submillimeter waves were line-of-sight, of course, but would ionosphere scatter make it possible for them to cover great distances? He could not remember. Or was that irrelevant, since perhaps they needed only to cover the distances between islands in their own archipelago? But then, why all the power? And in any case, what about this fantastic switching panel, hundreds of square feet of it even though it was transistorized and subminiaturized and involving at least a dozen sophisticated technical refinements he hadn't the training quite to understand? AT&T could have handled every phone call in the United States with less switching than this—in the days when telephone systems spanned a nation instead of a fraction of a city. He pushed the papers together in a pile and sat back, smoking a cigarette, trying to remember what he could of the theory behind submillimeter radiation.

At half a million megacycles and up the domain of quantum theory began to be invaded. Rotating gas molecules, constricted to a few energy states, responded directly to the radio waves. Chandler remembered late-night bull sessions in Pasadena during which it had been pointed out that the possibilities in the field were enormous—although only possibilities, for there was no engineering way to reach them, and no clear theory to point the way—suggesting such strange ultimate practical applications as the receiverless radio, for example. Was that what he had here?

He gave up. It was a question that would burn at him until he found the answer, but just now he had work to do, and he'd better be doing it. Skipping lunch entirely, he carefully checked the components lists, made a copy of what he would need, put the original envelope and its contents in the safe at the main receiving desk and caught the bus to Honolulu.

At the Parts 'n Plenty store, Hsi read the list with a faint frown that turned into a puzzled scowl. When he put it down he looked at Chandler for a few moments without speaking.

"Well, Hsi? Can you get all this for me?" The parts man shrugged and nodded. "Koitska said in three days."

Hsi looked startled, then resigned. "That puts it right up to me, doesn't it? All right. Wait a moment."

He disappeared in the back of the store, where Chandler heard him talking on what was evidently an intercom system. He came back in a few minutes and slipped Chandler's list into a slit in the locked door. "Tough for Bert," he said. "He'll be working all night, getting started—but I can take it easy till tomorrow. By then he'll know what we don't have, and I'll find some way to get it." He shrugged again, but his face was lined. Chandler wondered how one went about finding, for example, a thirty megawatt klystron tube; but it was Hsi's problem. He said:

"All right, I'll see you Monday."

"Wait a minute, Chandler." Hsi eyed him. "You don't have anything special to do, do you? Well, come have dinner with me. Maybe I can get to know you. Then maybe I can answer some of your questions, if you like."

They took a bus out Kapiolani Boulevard, then got out and walked a few blocks to a restaurant named Mother Chee's. Hsi was well known there, it seemed. He led Chandler to a booth at the back, nodded to the waiter, ordered without looking at the menu and sat back. "The food's all fish," he said. "You'll only find meat in the places where the Execs sometimes go.... Tell me something, Chandler. What's that scar on your forehead?"

Chandler touched it, almost with surprise. Since the medics had treated it he had almost forgotten it was there. He said, "What's the score? You testing me, too? Want to see if I'll lie about it?"

Hsi grinned. "Sorry. I guess that's what I was doing. I do know what an 'H' stands for; we've seen them before. Not many. The ones that do get this far usually don't last long. Unless, of course, they are working for somebody whom it wouldn't do to offend," he explained.

"So what you want to know, then, is whether I was really hoaxing or not. Does it make any difference?"

"Damn right it does, man! We're slaves, but we're not animals!" Chandler had gotten to him; the parts man looked startled, then sallow, as he observed his own vehemence.

"Sorry, Hsi. It makes a difference to me, too. Well, I wasn't hoaxing. I was possessed, just like any other everyday rapist, only I couldn't prove it. And it didn't look too good for me, because the damn thing happened in a pharmaceuticals plant. That was supposed to be about the only place in town where you could be sure you wouldn't be possessed, or so everybody thought. Including me. Up to the time I went ape."

Hsi nodded. The waiter approached with their drinks. Hsi looked at him appraisingly, then did a curious thing. He gripped his left wrist with his right hand, quickly, then released it again. The waiter did not appear to notice. Expertly he served the drinks, folded small pink floral napkins, dumped and wiped their ashtray in one motion—and then, so quickly that Chandler was not quite sure he had seen it, caught Hsi's wrist in the same fleeting gesture just before he turned and walked away.

Without comment Hsi turned back to Chandler. He said, "I believe you. Would you like to know why it happened? Because I think I can tell you. The Execs have all the antibiotics they need now."

"You mean—" Chandler hesitated.

"That's right. They did leave some areas alone, as long as they weren't fully stocked on everything they might want for the foreseeable future. Wouldn't you?"

"I might," Chandler said cautiously, "if I knew what I was—being an Exec."

Hsi said, "Eat your dinner. I'll take a chance and tell you what I know." He swallowed his whiskey-on-the-rocks wth a quick backward jerk of the head. "They're mostly Russians—you must know that much for yourself. The whole thing started in Russia."

Chandler said, "Well, that's pretty obvious. But Russia was smashed up as much as anywhere else. The whole Russian government was killed—wasn't it?"

Hsi nodded. "They're not the government. Not the Exec. Communism doesn't mean any more to them than the Declaration of Independence does—which is nothing. It's very simple, Chandler: they're a project that got out of hand."

Back three years ago, he said, in Russia, it started in the last days of the Second Stalinite Regime, before the neo-Khrushchevists took over power in the January Push.

The Western World had not known exactly what was going on, of course. Russia had become queerer and even more opaque after the Maoist trials and the revival of such fine old Soviet institutions as the Gay Pay Oo. That was the development called the Freeze, when the Stalinites seized control in the name of the sacred Generalissimo of the Soviet Fatherland, a mighty-missile party, dedicated to bringing about the world revolution by force of sputnik. The neo-Khrushchevists, on the other hand, believed that honey caught more flies than vinegar; and, although there were few visible adherents to that philosophy during the purges of the Freeze, they were not all dead. Then, out of the Donbas Electrical Workshop, came sudden support for their point of view.

It was a weapon. It was more than a weapon, an irresistible tool—more than that, the way to end all disputes forever.

It was a simple radio transmitter (Hsi said)—or so it seemed, but its frequencies were on an unusual band and its effects were remarkable. It controlled the minds of men. The "receiver" was the human brain. Through this little portable transmitter, surgically patch-wired to the brain of the person operating it, his entire personality was transmitted in a pattern of very short waves which could invade and modulate the personality of any other human being in the world.

"What's the matter?" Hsi interrupted himself, staring at Chandler. Chandler had stopped eating, his hand frozen midway to his mouth. He shook his head.

"Nothing. Go on." Hsi shrugged and continued.

While the Western World was celebrating Christmas—the Christmas before the first outbreak of possession in the outside world—the man who invented the machine was secretly demonstrating it to another man. Both of them were now dead; the inventor had been a Pole, the other man a former Party leader who, four years before, had pardoned the inventor's dying father from a Siberian work camp. The Party leader had reason to congratulate himself on that loaf cast on the water. There were only three

working models of the transmitter—what ultimately was
refined into the coronet Chandler had seen on the heads
of Koitska and the girl—but that was enough for the
January Push.

The Stalinites were out. The neo-Khrushchevists were
in.

A whole factory in the Donbas was converted to manu-
facturing these little mental controllers as fast as they could
be produced—and that was fast, for they were simple in
design to begin with and were quickly refined to a few
circuits. Even the surgical wiring to the brain became
unnecessary as induction coils tapped the encephalic
rhythms. Only the great amplifying hookup was really
complicated. Only one of those was necessary, for a single
amplifier could serve as rebroadcaster-modulator for thousands of the headsets.

"Are you sure you're all right?" Hsi demanded.

Chandler put down his fork, lit a cigarette and beckoned to the waiter. "I'm all right. I just want another
drink."

He needed it, for now he knew what he was building
for Koitska.

The waiter brought two more drinks and carried away
the uneaten food. "We don't know exactly who did what
after that," Hsi said, "but somehow or other it got out of
hand. I think it was the technical crew of the factory that
took over. I suppose it was an inevitable danger." He
grinned savagely. "I can just imagine the Party bosses in
the factory," he said, "trying to figure out how to keep the
workers in line—bribe them or terrify them? Give them
dachas or send a quota to Siberia? Neither would work, of
course, because there isn't any bribe you can give to a man
who only has to stretch out his hand to take over the
world, and you can't frighten a man who can make you slit
your own throat. Anyway, the next thing that happened—
the following Christmas—was when they took over the
world. It wasn't a Party movement at all any more. A lot
of the workers were Czechs and Hungarians and Poles,

and the first thing they wanted to do was to even a few scores.

"So here they are! Before they let the whole world go bang they got out of range. They got themselves out of Russia on two Red Navy cruisers, about a thousand of them; then they systematically triggered off every ballistic missile they could find . . . and they could find all of them, sooner or later, it was just a matter of looking. As soon as it was safe they moved in here.

"There are only a thousand or so of them here on the Islands, and nobody outside the Islands even knows where they are. If they did, what good would it do them? They can kill anyone, anywhere. They kill for fun, but sometimes they kill for a reason too. When one of them goes wandering for kicks he makes it a point to mess up all the transport and communications facilities he comes across—especially now, since they've stockpiled everything they're likely to need for the next twenty years. We don't know what they're planning to do when the twenty years are up. Maybe they don't care. Would you?"

Chandler drained his drink and shook his head. "One question," he said. "Who's 'we'?"

Hsi carefully unwrapped a package of cigarettes, took one out and lit it. He looked at it as though he were not enjoying it; cigarettes had a way of tasting stale these days. As they were. "Just a minute," he said.

Tardily Chandler remembered the quick grasp of the waiter's fingers on Hsi's wrist, and that the waiter had been hovering, inconspicuously close, all through their meal. Hsi was waiting for the man to return.

In a moment the waiter was back, looking directly at Chandler. He looped his own wrist with his fingers and nodded. Hsi said softly, " 'We' is the Society of Slaves. That's all of us—slaves—but only a few of us belong to the Society. We—"

There was a crash of glass. The waiter had dropped their tray.

Across the table from Chandler, Hsi looked suddenly changed. His left hand lay on the table before him, his right hand poised over it. Apparently he had been about to show Chandler again the sign he had made.

But he could not do it. His hand paused and fluttered like a captured bird. Captured it was. Hsi was captured. Out of Hsi's mouth, with Hsi's voice, came the light, tonal rhythms of Rosalie Pan: *"This* is an unexpected pleasure, love! I never expected to see you here. Enjoying your meal?"

Chandler had his empty glass halfway to his lips, automatically, before he realized there was nothing in it to brace him. He said hoarsely, "Yes, thanks. Do you come here often?" It was like the banal talk of a language handbook, wildly inappropriate to what had been going on a moment before. He was shaken.

"Oh, I love it," cooed Hsi, investigating the dishes before him. "All finished, I see. Too bad. Your friend doesn't feel like he ate much, either."

"I guess he wasn't hungry," Chandler managed.

"Well, I am." Hsi cocked his head and smiled like a clumsy female impersonator. "I know! Are you doing anything special right now, love? I know you've eaten, but—well, I've been a good girl and I guess I can eat a real meal, I mean not with somebody else's teeth, and still keep the calories in line. Suppose I meet you down at the beach? There's a place there where the luau is divine. I can be there in half an hour."

Chandler's breathing was back to normal. Why not? "I'll be delighted."

"Luigi the Wharf Rat, that's the name of it. They won't let you in, though, unless you tell them you're with me. It's—special." Hsi's eye closed in Rosalie Pan's wink. "Half an hour," he said, and was again himself.

He began to shake.

The waiter brought him straight whiskey and, pretense abandoned, stood by while Hsi drank it. After a moment he said, "Scares you. But—I guess we're all right. You'd better go, Chandler. I'll talk to you again some other time."

Chandler stood up. But he couldn't leave Hsi like that. "Are you all right?"

Hsi almost managed control. "Oh—I think so. Not the first time it's come close, you know. Sooner or later it'll come closer still and that will be the end, but—yes, I'm all right for now."

Chandler tarried. "You were saying something about the Society of Slaves."

"Damn it, go!" Hsi barked. "She'll be waiting for you. . . . Sorry, I didn't mean to shout. But go." As Chandler turned, he said more quietly, "Come around to the store tomorrow. Maybe we can finish our talk then."

XI

LUIGI THE Wharf Rat's was not actually on the beach but on the bank of a body of water called the Ala Wai Canal. Across the water were the snowtopped hills. A maitre-d' escorted Chandler personally to a table on a balcony, and there he waited. Rosalie's "half-hour" was nearly two; but then he heard her calling him from across the room, in the voice which had reached a thousand second balconies, and he rose as she came near.

She said lightly, "Sorry. You ought to be flattered, though. It's a twenty-minute drive—and an hour and a half to put on my face, so you won't be ashamed to be seen with me. Well, it's good to be out in my own skin for a change. Let's eat!"

The talk with Hsi had left a mark on Chandler that not even this girl's pretty face could obscure. It was a pretty face, though, and she was obviously exerting herself to make him enjoy himself. He could not help responding to her mood.

She talked of her life on the stage, the excitement of a

performance, the entertainers she had known. Her conversation was one long name-drop, but it was not vanity: the world of the famous was the world she had lived in. It was not a world that Chandler had ever visited, but he recognized the names. Rosie had been married once to an English actor whose movies Chandler had made a point of watching on television. It was interesting, in a way, to know that the man snored and lived principally on vitamin pills. But it was a view of the man that Chandler had not sought.

The restaurant drew its clientele mostly from the Execs, young ones or young-acting ones, like the girl. The coronets were all over. There had been a sign on the door:

KAPU, WALIHINI!

to mark it off limits to anyone not an exec or a collaborator. Still, Chandler thought, who on the island was not a collaborator? The only effective resistance a man could make would be to kill everyone within reach and then himself, thus depriving them of slaves—and that was, after all, only what the Execs themselves had done in other places often enough. It would inconvenience them only slightly. The next few planeloads or shiploads of possessed warm bodies from the mainland would be permitted to live, instead of being required to dash themselves to destruction, like the crew of the airplane that had carried Chandler. Thus the domestic stocks would be replenished.

An annoying feature of dining with Rosalie in the flesh, Chandler found, was that half a dozen times while they were talking he found himself taken, speaking words to Rosie that were not his own, usually in a language he did not understand. She took it as a matter of course; it was merely a friend, across the room or across the island, using Chandler as the casual convenience of a telephone. "Sorry," she apologized blithely after it happened for the third time. "You don't like that, love, do you?"

"Can you blame me?" He stopped himself from saying more; he was astonished even so at his tone.

She said it for him. "I know. It takes away your manhood, I suppose. Please don't let it do that to you, love. We're not so bad. Even—" She hesitated, and did not go on. "You know," she said, "I came here the same way you did. Kidnapped off the stage of the Winter Garden. Of course, the difference was the one who kidnapped me was an old friend. Though I didn't know it at the time and it scared me half to death."

Chandler must have looked startled. She nodded. "You've been thinking of us as another race, haven't you? Like the Neanderthals or—well, worse than that, maybe." She smiled. "We're not. About half of us came from Russia in the first place, but the others are from all over. You'd be astonished, really." She mentioned several names, world-famous scientists, musicians, writers. "Of course, not everybody can qualify for the club, love. Wouldn't be exclusive otherwise. The chief rule is loyalty. I'm loyal," she added gently after a moment, "and don't you forget it. Have to be. Whoever becomes an exec has to be with us, all the way. There are tests. It has to be that way—not only for our protection. For the world's."

Chandler was genuinely startled at that. Rosie nodded seriously. "If one exec should give away something he's not supposed to, it would upset the whole applecart. There are only a thousand of us, and I guess probably two billion of you, or nearly. The result would be complete destruction."

Of the Executive Committee, Chandler thought she meant at first, but then he thought again. No. Of the world. For the thousand execs, outnumbered though they were two million to one, could not fail to triumph. The contest would not be in doubt. If the whole thousand execs at once began systematically to kill and destroy, instead of merely playing at it as the spirit moved them, they could all but end the human race overnight. A man could be made to slash his throat in a quarter of a minute. An exec, killing, killing, killing without pause, could destroy his own two million enemies in an eight-hour day.

And there were surer, faster ways. Chandler did not have to imagine them, he had seen them. The massacre of the Orphalese, the victims at the Monument—they were only crumbs of destruction. What had happened to New York City showed what mass-production methods could do. No doubt there were bombs left, even if only chemical ones. Shoot, stab, crash, blow up; swallow poison, leap from window, slit throat. Every man a murderer, at the touch of a mind from Hawaii; and if no one else was near to murder, surely each man could find a victim in himself. In one ravaging day mankind would cease to exist as a major force. In a week the only survivors would be those in such far off and hopelessly impotent places that they were not worth the trouble of tracking down.

"You hate us, don't you?"

Chandler paused and tried to find an answer. Rosie was neither belligerent nor mocking. She was only sympathetically trying to reach his point of view. He shook his head.

"Not meaning 'no'—meaning 'no comment?' Well, I don't blame you, love. But do you see that we're not altogether a bad thing? Until we came along the world was getting ready to kill itself anyway."

"There's a difference," Chandler mumbled. He was thinking of his wife. He and Margot had loved each other as married couples do—without any very great, searing compulsion; but with affection, with habit and with sporadic passion. Chandler had not given much thought to the whole, though he was aware of the parts, during the last years of his marriage. It was only after Margot's murder that he had come to know that the sum of those parts was a quite irreplaceable love.

But Rosie was shaking her head. "The difference is all on our side. Suppose Koitska's boss had never discovered the coronets. At any moment one country might have got nervous and touched off the whole thing—not carefully, the way we did it, with most of the really dirty missiles fused safe and the others landing where they were supposed to go. I mean, touched off a *war*. The end, love. The bloody *finis*. The ones that were killed at once would have been the lucky ones. No, love," she said, in dead earnest, "we aren't the worst things that ever happened to the world. Once the bad part is over, people will understand what we really are."

"And what's that, exactly?"

She hesitated, smiled and said modestly, "We're gods."

It took Chandler's breath away—not because it was untrue, but because it had never occurred to him that gods were aware of their divinity.

"We're gods, love, with the privilege of electing mortals to the club. Don't judge us by anything that has gone before. Don't judge us by anything. We are a New Thing. We don't have to conform to precedent because we upset all precedents. From now on, to the end of time, the rules will grow from us."

She patted her lips briskly with a napkin and said, "Would you like to see something? Let's take a little walk."

She took him by the hand and led him across the room, out to a sundeck on the other side of the restaurant. They were looking down on what had once been a garden. There were people in it; Chandler was conscious of sounds coming from them, and he was able to see that there were dozens of them, perhaps a hundred, and that they all seemed to be wearing suntans like his own.

"From Tripler?" he guessed.

"No, love. They pick out those clothes themselves. Stand there a minute."

The girl in the coronet walked out to the rail of the sundeck, where pink and amber spotlights were playing on nothing. As she came into the colored lights there was a sigh from the people in the garden. A man walked forward with an armload of leis and deposited them on the ground below the rail.

They were *adoring* her.

Rosalie stood gravely for a moment, then nodded and returned to Chandler.

"They began doing that about a year ago," she whispered to him, as a murmur of disappointment came up from the crowd. "Their own idea. We didn't know what they wanted at first, but they weren't doing any harm. You see, love," she said softly, "we can make them do anything we like. But we don't make them do that."

Hours later, Chandler was not sure just how, they were in a light plane flying high over the Pacific, clear out of sight of land. The moon was gold above them, the ocean black beneath.

Chandler stared down as the girl circled the plane, slipping lower toward the water, silent and perplexed. But he was not afraid. He was almost content. Rosie was good company—gay, cheerful—and she had treasures to share. It had been an impulse of hers, a long drive in her sports car and a quick, comfortable flight over the ocean to cap the evening. It had been a pleasant impulse. He reflected gravely that he could understand now how generations of country maidens had been dazzled and despoiled. A touch of luxury was a great seducer.

The coronet on the girl's body could catch his body at any moment. She had only to think herself into his mind, and her will, flashed to a relay station like the one he was building for Koitska, at loose in infinity, could sweep into him and make him a puppet. If she chose, he would open that door beside him and step out into a thousand feet of air and a meal for the sharks.

But he did not think she would do it. He did not think anyone would, really, though with his own eyes he had seen some anyones do things as bad as that and sickeningly worse. There was not a corrupt whim of the most diseased mind in history that some torpid exec had not visited on a helpless man, woman or child in the past years. Even as they flew here, Chandler knew, the gross bodies that lay in luxury in the island's villas were surging restlessly around the world; and death and shame remained where they had passed.

It was a paradox too great to be reconciled, this girl and this vileness. He could not forget it, but he could not feel it in his glands. She was pretty. She was gay. He began to think thoughts that had left him alone for a long time.

The dark bulk of the island showed ahead and they were sinking toward a landing.

The girl landed skillfully on a runway that sprang into light as she approached—electronic wizardry, or the coronet and some tethered serf at a switch? It didn't matter. Nothing mattered very greatly at that moment to Chandler.

"Thank you, love," she said, laughing. "I liked that. It's all very well to use someone else's body for this sort of thing, but every now and then I want to keep my own in practice."

She linked arms with him as they left the plane. "When I was first given the coronet here," she reminisced, amusement in her voice, "I got the habit real bad. I spent six awful months—really, six months in bed! And by myself at that. Oh, I was all over the world, and skin-diving on the Barrier Reef and skiing in Norway and—well," she said, squeezing his arm, "never *mind* what all. And then one day I got on the scales, just out of habit. Do you know what I *weighed?*" She closed her eyes in mock horror, but they were smiling when she opened them again. "I won't do that again, love. Of course, a lot of us do let ourselves go. Even Koitska. Especially Koitska. And some of the women— But just between us, the ones who do really didn't have much to keep in shape in the first place."

She led the way into a villa that smelled of jasmine and gardenias, snapped her fingers and subdued lights came on. "Like it? Oh, we've nothing but the best. What would you like to drink?"

She fixed them both tall, cold glasses and vetoed Chandler's choice of a sprawling wicker chair to sit on. "Over here, love." She patted the couch beside her. She drew up her legs, leaning against him, very soft, warm and fragrant, and said dreamily, "Let me see. What's nice? What do you like in music, love?"

"Oh . . . anything."

"No, no! You're supposed to say, 'Why, the original-cast album from *Fancy Free.*' Or anything else I starred in." She shook her head reprovingly, and the points of her coronet caught golden reflections from the lights. "But since you're obviously a man of low taste I'll have to do the whole bit myself." She touched switches at a remote-control set by her end of the couch, and in a moment dreamy strings began to come from tri-aural speakers hidden around the room. It was not *Fancy Free.* "That's better," she said drowsily, and in a moment, "Wasn't it nice in the plane?"

"It was fine," Chandler said. Gently—but firmly—he sat up and reached automatically into his pocket.

The girl sighed and straightened. "Cigarette? They're on the table beside you. Hope you like the brand. They only keep one big factory going, not to count those terrible Russian things that're all air and no smoke." She touched his forehead with cool fingers. "You never told me about that, love."

It was like an electric shock—the touch of her fingers and the touch of reality at once. Chandler said stiffly, "My brand. But I thought you were there."

"Oh, only now and then. I missed all the naughty parts—though, to tell the truth, that's why I was hanging around. I do like to hear a little naughtiness now and then . . . but all I heard was that stupid lawyer and that stupid judge. Made me mad." She giggled. "Lucky for you. I was so irritated I decided to spoil their fun too."

Chandler sat up and took a long pull at his drink. Curiously, it seemed to sober him. He said: "It's nothing. I happened to rape a young girl. Happens every day. Of course, it was one of your friends that was doing it for me, but I didn't miss any of what was going on, I can give you a blow-by-blow description if you like. The people in the town where I lived, at that time, thought I was doing it on my own, though, and they didn't approve. Hoaxing—you know? They thought I was so perverse and cruel that I would do that sort of thing under my own power, instead of with some exec—or, as they would have put it, being ignorant, some imp, or devil, or demon—pulling the strings."

He was shaking. He waited for what she had to say; but she only whispered, "I'm sorry, love," and looked so contrite and honest that, as rapidly as it had come upon him, his anger passed.

He opened his mouth to say something to her. He didn't get it said. She was sitting there, looking at him, alone and soft and inviting. He kissed her; and as she returned the kiss, he kissed her again, and again.

But less than an hour later he was in her Porsche, cold sober, raging, frustrated, miserable. He slammed it through the unfamiliar gears as he sped back to the city.

She had left him. They had kissed with increasing passion, his hands playing about her, her body surging toward him, and then, just then, she whispered, "No, love." He held her tighter and without another word she opened her eyes and looked at him.

He knew what mind it was that caught him then. It was her mind. Stiffly, like wood, he released her, stood up, walked to the door and locked it behind him.

The lights in the villa went out. He stood there, boiling, looking into the shadows through the great, wide, empty window. He could see her lying there on the couch, and as he watched he saw her body toss and stir; and as surely as he had ever known anything before he knew that somewhere in the world some woman—or some man!—lay locked with a lover, violent in love, and was unable to tell the other that a third party had invaded their bed.

Chandler did not know it until he saw something glistening on his wrist, but he was weeping on the wild ride back to Honolulu in the car. Her car. Would there be trouble for his taking it? God, let there be trouble! He was in a mood for trouble. He was sick and wild with revulsion.

Worse than her use of him, a casual stimulant, an aphrodisiac touch, was that she thought what she did was right. Chandler thought of the worshipping dozens under the sundeck of the exec restaurant, and Rosalie's gracious benediction as they made her their floral offerings. Blind, pathetic fools!

Not only the deluded men and women in the garden were worshippers trapped in a vile religion, he thought. It was worse. The gods and goddesses worshipped at their own divinity as well!

XII

THREE DAYS later Koitska's voice, coming from Chandler's lips, summoned him out to the TWA shack again.

Wise now in the ways of this world, Chandler commandeered a police car and was hurried out to the South Gate, where the guards allowed him a car of his own. The door of the building was unlocked and Chandler went right up.

He was astonished. The fat man was actually sitting up. He was fully dressed—more or less; incongruously he wore flowered shorts and a bright red, short-sleeve shirt, with rope sandals. His coronet perched on his plump old head; curiously, he carried another, less ornate one. He said, "You fly a *gilikopter*? No? No difference. Help me." An arm like a mountain went over Chandler's shoulders. The man must have weighed three hundred pounds. Slowly, wheezing, he limped toward the back of the room and touched a button.

A door opened.

Chandler had not known before that there was an elevator in the building; that was one of the things the Exec did not consider important for his slaves to know. The elevator lowered them with great grace and delicacy to the first floor, where a large old Cadillac, ancient but immaculately kept, the kind that used to be called a "gangster's car," waited in a private parking bay.

Chandler followed Koitska's directions and drove to an airfield where a small, Plexiglass-nosed helicopter waited. More by the force of Chandler pushing him from behind than through his own fat thighs, Koitska puffed up the little staircase into the cabin. Originally the copter had been fitted for four passengers. Now there was the pilot's seat and a seat beside it, and in the back a wide, soft couch. Koitska collapsed onto it, clutching the extra coronet. His face blanked out—he was, Chandler knew, somewhere else, just then.

In a moment his eyes opened again. He looked at Chandler with no interest at all, and turned his face to the wall.

After a moment he wheezed. "Sit down. At de controls." He breathed noisily for a while. Then, "It von't pay you to be interested in Rosalie," he said.

Chandler was startled. He craned around in the seat but saw only Koitska's back. "I'm not! Or anyway—" But he had no place to go in that sentence, and in any case Koitska no longer seemed interested.

After a moment, Koitska stirred, settled himself more comfortably—and Chandler felt himself taken.

He turned, easily and surely, to face the split wheel and the unfamiliar pedals of the helicopter. He started the motor, scanned the panels of instruments, and through maneuvers which he did not understand but whose effect was accurate and sure, caused the machine to roar, tilt and whir up and away. It was an admirable performance. Chandler could not guess what member of the Exec was inhabiting his body at that moment; there were no clues; but whoever it was, it had turned him into a first-class helicopter pilot.

For more than an hour Chandler was imprisoned in his own body, without let or intermission. Flying a helicopter, it seemed, was a job without coffee breaks. The remote exec who was controlling him did not trust his attention away even for a moment.

It was like being the prisoner of a dream, thought Chandler, watching his right hand advance a throttle and his feet press the guiding pedals. From time to time his head turned and his voice spoke over his shoulder to Koitska; but as the conversation seemed to be in Russian or Polish he gleaned nothing from it. There was not much talk, though; the fluttering roar of the vanes overhead drowned out most sounds. Chandler fell into a light, somber, not unpleasant reverie, thinking of Ellen Braisted and the Orphalese, of the girl Rosalie Pan and the fat, murderous slug behind him. It occurred to him, as a phenomenon worthy of study, that he was actually aiding and abetting the monsters who had destroyed his own wife and caused him to defile a silly but blameless girl. . . .

The moral issues were too deep for him. He preferred to think of Rosalie Pan, and then of nothing at all.

They crossed a wide body of ocean and approached another island; from one quick glance at a navigation map that his eyes had taken, Chandler guessed it to be Hilo. He landed the craft expertly on the margin of a small airstrip, where two DC-3s were already parked and being unloaded, and felt himself free again.

Two husky young men, apparently native Hawaiians by their size, rolled up a ramp and assisted Koitska down it and into a building. Chandler was left to his own devices. The building was rundown but sound. Around it stalky grass clumped, long uncut, and a few mauve and scarlet blossoms, almost hidden, showed where someone had once tended beds of bougainvillea and poinsettias.

He could not guess what the building had been doing there, looking like a small office-factory combination out in the remote wilds, until he caught sight of a sign the winds had blown against a wall: *Dole.* Apparently this had been headquarters for one of the plantations. Now it was stripped almost clean inside, a welter of desks and rusted machines piled heedlessly outside where there once had been a parking lot. New equipment was being loaded into it from the cargo planes. Chandler recognized some of it as from the list he had given the parts man, Hsi. There also seemed to be a gasoline-driven generator—a large one— but what the other things were he could not guess.

Besides Koitska, there were at least five coronet-wearing execs visible around the place. Chandler was not surprised. It would have to be something big to winkle these torpid slugs out of their shells, but he knew what it was, and that it was big enough to them indeed.

In fact it was their lives. He deduced that Koitska's plans for his future comfort required a standby transmitter to service the coronets, in case something went wrong— perhaps a slightly modified one, judging by the extra coronet Koitska had brought. And clearly it was this that they were to put together here.

For ten hours, while the afternoon became dark night, they worked at a furious pace. When the sun set one of the execs gestured and the generator was started, rocking on its rubber-tired wheels as its rotors spun and fumes chugged out, and they worked on by strings of incandescent lights.

It was pick-and-shovel work for Chandler. No engineering, just unloading and roughly grouping the equipment where it was ready to be assembled. The execs did not take part in the work. Nor were they idle. They busied themselves in one room of the building with some small device—Chandler could not see what—and when he looked again it was gone. He did not see them take it away and did not know where it was taken. Toward midnight he suddenly realized that it was likely some essential part which they would not permit anyone but themselves to handle . . . and that, no doubt, was why they had come in person, instead of working through proxies.

Weary as he was, that realization seemed pregnant with possibilities to Chandler. What could be so important? And what use could he make of the information? So much had happened to Chandler, so quickly, that he seemed to have numbed his reflexes. He was not reacting as rapidly or as surely as he should; in this Wonderland if the Red

Queen were to come up to him and lop off his head he might not even remember to die. Dizzying, worrying—his sensory network simply could not cope with the demands on it. But all the same, he thought slowly and painfully, there was a weapon here, a lever. . . .

Just before they left Koitska and two or three of the other execs quizzed him briefly.

He was too tired to think beyond the questions, but they seemed to be trying to find out if he were able to do the simpler parts of the construction without supervision, and they seemed satisfied with the answers. He flew the helicopter home, with someone else guiding his arms and legs, but he was half asleep as he did it, and he never quite remembered how he managed to get back to his room at Tripler.

The next morning he went back to Parts 'n Plenty with an additional list, covering replacement of some components that had turned out defective. Hsi glanced at it quickly and nodded. "All this stuff I have. You can pick it up this afternoon if you like."

Chandler offered him a cigarette out of a stale pack. "About the other night—"

But Hsi shook his head violently. He began to perspire, but he said, casually enough, "Interested in baseball?"

"Baseball?"

Hsi said, as though there had been nothing incongruous about the question, "Why, there's a little league game this afternoon. Back of the school on Punahou and Wilder. I thought I might stop by, then we can come back and pick up the rest of your gear. Two o'clock. Hope I'll see you."

Chandler walked away thoughtfully. Something in Hsi's attitude suggested more than a ball game; after a quick and poor lunch he decided to go.

The field was a dirty playground, scuffed out of what had probably once been an attractive campus. The players were ten-year-olds, of the mixture of hair colors and complexions typical of the islands. Chandler was puzzled

Surely even the wildest baseball rooter wouldn't go far out of his way for this, and yet there was an audience of at least fifty adults watching the game. And none seemed to be related to the ballplayers. The little leaguers played grave, careful ball, and the audience watched them without a word of parental encouragement or joy.

Hsi approached him from the shadow of the school building. "Glad you could make it, Chandler. No, no questions. Just watch."

In the fifth inning, with the score aggregating around thirty, there was an interruption. A tall, red-headed man glanced at his watch, licked his lips, took a deep breath and walked out onto the diamond. He glanced at the crowd, while the kids suspended play without surprise. Then the red-headed man nodded to the umpire and stepped off the field. The ballplayers resumed their game, but now the whole attention of the audience was on the red-headed man.

Suspicion crossed Chandler's mind. In a moment it was confirmed, as the red-headed man raised his hands waist high and clasped his right hand around his left wrist—only for a moment, but that was enough.

The ball game was a cover. Chandler was present at a meeting of what Hsi had called The Society of Slaves, the underground that dared to pit itself against the Execs.

Hsi cleared his throat and said, "This is the one. I vouch for him." And that was startling too, Chandler thought, because all these wrist-circled men and women were looking at *him*.

"All right," said the red-headed man nervously, "let's get started then. First thing, anybody got any weapons? Sure? Take a look—we don't want any slip-ups. Turn out your pockets."

There was a flurry and a woman near Chandler held up a key ring with a tiny knife on it. "Penknife? Hell, yes; get rid of it. Throw it in the outfield. You can pick it up after the meeting." A hundred eyes watched the pearly object fly. "We ought to be all right here," said the red-headed man. "The kids have been playing every day this week and nobody looked in. But *watch your neighbor*. See anything suspicious, don't wait. Don't take a chance. Holler 'Kill the umpire!' or anything you like, but holler. Good and loud." He paused, breathing hard. "All right, Hsi. Introduce him."

The parts man took Chandler firmly by the shoulder. "This fellow has something for us," he said. "He's working for the Exec Koitska, building what can't be anything else but a duplicate of the machine that they use to control us!"

Chandler was jolted out of his detached calm. "Hey!" he cried. "I never said anything like that!"

"You didn't have to," Hsi said tightly. "What the hell do you think I am, an idiot? I've filled all your parts orders, remember? It's higher frequency, but otherwise it's a duplicate of the master transmitter."

"But they never told me—"

"*Told* you? Did they have to tell you? What else would they be so busy at?"

Chandler hesitated, staring around. The words had been actually frightening. And yet—and yet, he realized, he had been sure within himself that the project he was working on was something very like that. A duplicate of the controlling machine. And that meant—

A tall, thin, bearded man was moving forward, staring at Chandler angrily. He said dangerously, "You don't seem too reliable, friend. Which side are you on?"

Chandler shrugged. "Why—yours, of course, I guess. I mean—"

"You guess, huh?" The man nodded, then leaned forward and peered furiously into Chandler's face. "Look at his head!" he cried, his face only inches away from Chandler's own. "Don't you see? He's branded!"

Chandler fell back, touching his scar. The man followed. "Damned Hoaxer! Look at him! The lowest species of life on the face of the earth—someone who pretended to be possessed in order to do some damned dirty act. What was it, hoaxer? Murder? Burning babies alive?"

Hsi economically let go of Chandler's shoulder, half turned the bearded man with one hand and swung with the other, knocking him down. "Shut up, Linton. Wait till you hear what he's got for us."

The bearded man, sprawling and groggy, slowly rose as Hsi explained tersely what he had guessed of Chandler's work—as much as Chandler himself knew, it seemed. "Maybe this is only a duplicate. Maybe it won't be used. But maybe it will—and Chandler's the man who can sabotage it! How would you like that? The Exec switching over to this equipment while the other one is down for maintenance—and their headsets don't work!"

There was a terrible silence, except for the sounds of the children playing ball. Two runs had just scored. Chandler recognized the silence. It was hope.

Linton broke it, his blue eyes gleaming above the beard. "No! Better than that. Why wait? We can *use* this fellow's machine. Set it up, get us some headsets—and we can control the Execs themselves!"

The silence was even longer; then there was a babble of discussion, but Chandler did not take part in it. He was thinking. It was a tremendous thought.

Suppose a man like himself were actually able to do what they wanted of him. Never mind the practical difficulties—learning how it worked, getting a headset, bypassing the traps Koitska would surely have set to prevent just that. Never mind the penalties for failure. Suppose he could make it work, and find fifty headsets, and fit them to the fifty men and women here in this clandestine meeting of The Society of Slaves . . .

Would there, after all, be any change worth mentioning in the state of the world?

Or was Lord Acton, always and everywhere, right? Power corrupts. Absolute power corrupts absolutely. The power locked in the coronets of the Exec was more than flesh and blood could stand; he could almost sense the rot in those near him at the mere thought.

But Hsi was throwing cold water on the idea. "Sorry, but I know that much: One exec can't control another. The headpieces insulate against control. Well." He glanced at his watch. "We agreed on twenty minutes maximum for this meeting," he reminded the red-headed man, who nodded.

"You're right." He glanced around the group. "I'll make the rest of it fast. News: You all know they got some more of us last week. Have you all been by the Monument? Three of our comrades were still there this morning. But I don't think they know we're organized, they think it's only individual acts of sabotage. In case any of you don't know, the execs can't read our minds. Not even when they're controlling us. Proof is we're all still alive. Hanrahan knew practically every one of us, and he's been lying out there for a week with a broken back, ever since they caught him trying to blow up the guard pits at East Gate. They had plenty of chance to pump him if they could. *They can't.* Next thing. No more individual attacks on one exec. Not unless it's a matter of life and death, and even then you're wasting your time unless you've got a gun. They can grab your mind faster than you can cut a throat. Third thing: Don't get the idea there are good execs and bad execs. Once they put that thing on their heads they're all the same. Fourth thing. You can't make deals. They aren't that worried. So if anybody's thinking of selling out—I'm not saying anyone is—forget it." He looked around. "Anything else?"

"What about germ warfare in the water supply?" somebody ventured.

"Still looking into it. No report yet. All right, that's enough for now. Meeting's adjourned. Watch the ball game for a while, then drift away. *One at a time.*"

Hsi was the first to go, then a couple of women, together, then a sprinkling of other men. Chandler, still numbed by the possibility that had opened before him, was in no particular hurry, although it seemed time to leave anyway. The ball game appeared to be over. A ten-year-old with freckles on his face was at the plate, but he was leaning on his bat, staring at Chandler with wide, serious eyes.

Chandler felt a sudden chill.

He turned, began to walk away—and felt himself seized.

He walked slowly into the schoolhouse, unable to look around. Behind him he heard a confused sob, tears and a child's voice trying to blubber through: "Something *funny* happened."

If the child had been an adult it might have been warning enough. But the child had never experienced possession before, was not sure enough, was not clear enough. Chandler was clear into the schoolhouse before the remaining members of The Society of Slaves awoke to their danger. He heard a quick cry of *They got him!* Then Chandler's legs stopped walking and he addressed himself savagely. A few yards away a stout Chinese lady was mopping the tiles; she looked up at him, startled, but no more startled than Chandler was himself. "You idiot!" Chandler blazed. "Why do you have to get mixed up in this? Don't you know it's wrong, love? Stay here!" Chandler commanded himself. "Don't you *dare* leave this building!"

And he was free again, but there was a sudden burst of screams from outside.

Bewildered, Chandler stood for a moment, as little able to move as though the girl still had him under control. Then he leaped through a classroom to a window, staring. Outside in the playground there was wild confusion. Half the spectators were on the ground, trying to rise. As he watched, a teen-age boy hurled himself at an elderly lady, the two of them falling. Another man flung himself to the ground. A woman swung her pocketbook into the face of the man next to her. One of the fallen ones rose, only to trip himself again. It was a mad spectacle, but Chandler understood it: What he was watching was a single member of the execs trying to keep a group of twenty ordinary, un-armed human beings in line. The exec was leaping from mind to mind; even so, the crowd was beginning to scatter.

Without thought Chandler started to leap out to help them; but the possessor had anticipated that. He was caught at the door. He whirled and ran toward the wom-an with the mop; as he was released, the woman flung herself upon him, knocking him down.

By the time he was able to get up again it was far too late to help . . . if there ever had been a time when he could have helped.

He heard shots. Two policemen had come running into the playground, guns drawn.

The exec who had looked at him out of the boy's eyes, who had penetrated this nest of enemies and extricated Chandler from it, had taken first things first. Help had been summoned. Quick as the coronets worked, it was no time at all until the nearest persons with weapons were located, commandeered and in action.

Two minutes later there no longer was resistance.

Obviously more execs had come to help, attracted by the commotion perhaps, or summoned at some stolen moment after the meeting had first been invaded. There were only five survivors on the field. Each was clearly controlled. They rose and stood patiently while the two police shot them, shot them, paused to reload and shot again. The last to die was the bearded man, Linton, and as he fell his eyes brushed Chandler's.

Chandler leaned against a wall.

It had been a terrible sight. The nearness of his own death had been almost the least of it. Far worse, far more damaging—and how many times had it tortured him now?—was the death of hope. For one moment there he had seen a vision of freedom again. Him on the island of Hilo, somehow magically gimmicking the controlling ma-chine that gave the Executive Committee its power, here in Honolulu the Society of Slaves somehow magically using the hour of freedom he gave them to destroy their oppressors. . . .

But it was all gone now, and it would not come again.

His own escape was both miraculous and, very likely, only a temporary thing. He had no doubt of the identity of the exec who had interfered to save him . . . and had destroyed the others. Though he had heard the voice only as it came from his own mouth, he could not mistake it. It was Rosalie Pan.

He looked out at the red-headed man, sprawled across the foul line behind third base, and remembered what he said. There weren't any good execs or bad execs. There were only execs.

XIII

WHATEVER CHANDLER'S life might be worth, he knew he had given it away and the girl had given it back to him.

He did not see her for several days, but the morning after the massacre he woke to find a note beside his bed table. No one had been in the room. It was his own sleeping hand that had written it, though the girl's mind had moved his fingers:

> If you get mixed up in anything like that again I won't be able to help you. So don't! Those people are just using you, you know. Don't throw away your chances. Do you like surfboarding?
>
>   Rosie

But by then there was no time for surfboarding, or for anything else but work. The construction job on Hilo had begun, and it was a nightmare. He was flown to the island with the last load of parts. No execs were present in the flesh, but on the first day Chandler lost count of how many different minds possessed his own. He began to be able to recognize them by a limp as he walked, by tags of German as he spoke, by a stutter, a distinctive gesture of annoyance, an expletive. As he was a trained engineer he was left to labor by himself for hours on end; it was worse for the others in the construction crew. There seemed to be a dozen execs hovering invisible around all the time; no sooner was a worker released by one than he was seized by another. The work progressed rapidly, but at the cost of utter exhaustion.

By the end of the fourth day Chandler had eaten only two meals and could not remember when he had slept last. He found himself staggering when free and furious with the fatigue-clumsiness of his own body when possessed. At sundown on the fourth day he found himself free for a moment and, incredibly, without work of his own to do just then, until someone else completed a job of patch-wiring. He stumbled out into the open air and had time only to gaze around for a moment before his eyes began to close. He had time to think that this must once have been a lovely island. Even unkempt as it was the trees were tall and beautiful; beyond them a wisp of smoke was pale against the dark-blue evening sky; the breeze was scented. . . . He woke and found he was already back in the building, reaching for his soldering gun.

There came a point at which even the will of the execs was unable to drive the flogged bodies farther, and then they were permitted to sleep for a few hours. At daybreak they were awake again.

The sleep was not enough. The bodies were slow and inaccurate. Two of the Hawaiians, straining a hundred-pound component into place, staggered, slipped—and dropped it.

Appalled, Chandler waited for them to kill themselves.

But it seemed that the execs were tiring too. One of the Hawaiians said irritably, with an accent Chandler did not recognize: "That's pau. All right, you morons, you've won yourselves a vacation; we'll have to fly you in replacements. Take the day off." And incredibly all eleven of the haggard wrecks stumbling around the building were free at once.

The first thought of every man was to eat, to relieve himself, to remove a shoe and ease a blistered foot—to do any of the things they had not been permitted to do. The second thought was sleep.

Chandler dropped off at once, but he was over-tired; he slept fitfully, and after an hour or two of turning on the hard ground, sat up, blinking red-eyed around. He had been slow. The cushioned seats in the aircraft and cars were already taken. He stood up, stretched, scratched himself and wondered what to do next, and he remembered the thread of smoke he had seen—when? three nights ago?—against the evening sky.

In all those hours he had not had time to think one obvious thought: There should have been no smoke there! The island was supposed to be deserted.

It was of no importance, of course. What could it matter to him? But he had nothing else to do. He stood up, looked around to get his bearings, and started off in the direction he remembered.

It was good to own his body again, in poor condition as it was. It was delicious to be allowed to think consecutive thoughts.

The chemistry of the human animal is such that it heals whatever thrusts it may receive from the outside world. Short of death, its only incapacitating wound comes from itself; from the outside it can survive astonishing blows, rise again, and flourish. Chandler was not flourishing, but he had begun to rise.

Time had been so compressed and blurred in the days since the slaughter at the Punahou School that he had not had time to grieve over the deaths of his briefly met friends, or even to think of their quixotic plans against the execs. Now he began to wonder.

He understood with what thrill of hope he had been received—a man like themselves, not an exec, whose touch was at the very center of the exec power. But how firm was that touch? Was there really anything he could do?

It seemed not. He barely understood the mechanics of what he was doing, far less the theory behind it. Conceivably knowing where this installation was he could somehow get back to it when it was completed. In theory it might be that there was a way to dispense with the headsets and exert power from the big board itself.

A Piltdowner at the controls of a nuclear-laden jet bomber could destroy a city. Nothing stopped him. Nothing but his own invincible ignorance. Chandler was that Piltdowner; certainly power was here to grasp, but he had no way of knowing how to pick it up.

Still—where there was life there was hope. He decided he was wasting time that would not come again. He had been wandering along a road that led into a small town, quite deserted, but this was no time for wandering. His place was back at the installation, studying, scheming, trying to understand all he could. He began to turn, and stopped.

"Great God," he sad softly, looking at what he had just seen. The town was deserted of life, but not of death.

There were bodies everywhere.

They were long dead, perhaps years. They seemed natural and right as they lay there; it was not surprising they had escaped his notice at first. Little was left but bones and an occasional desiccated leathery rag that might have been a face. The clothing was faded and rotted away; but enough was left of the bodies and the clothes to make it clear that none of these people had died natural deaths. A rusted blade in a chest cage showed where a knife had pierced a heart; a small skull near his feet (with a scrap of faded blue rompers near it) was shattered. On a flagstone terrace a family group of bones lay radiating outward, like a rosette. Something had exploded there and caught them all as they turned to flee. There was a woman's face, grained like oak and eyeless, visible between the fender of a truck and a crushed-in wall.

Like exhumed Pompeii, the tragedy was so ancient that it aroused only wonder. The whole town had been blotted out.

The Execs did not take chances; apparently they had sterilized the whole island—probably had sterilized all of them except Oahu itself, to make certain that their isolation was complete, except for the captive stock allowed to breed and serve them in and around Honolulu.

Chandler prowled the town for a quarter of an hour, but one street was like another. The bodies did not seem to have been disturbed even by animals, but perhaps there were none big enough to show traces of such work.

Something moved in a doorway.

Chandler thought at once of the smoke he had seen, but no one answered his call and, though he searched, he could neither see nor hear anything alive.

The search was a waste of time. It also wasted his best chance to study the thing he was building. As he returned to the cinder-block structure at the end of the airstrip he heard motors and looked up to see a plane circling in for a landing.

He knew that he had only a few minutes. He spent those minutes as thriftily as he could, but long before he could even grasp the circuitry of the parts he had not himself worked on he felt a touch at his mind. The plane was rolling to a stop. He and all of them hurried over to begin unloading it.

The plane was stopped with one wingtip almost touching the building, heading directly into it—convenient for unloading, but a foolish nuisance when it came time to turn it and take off again, Chandler's mind thought while his body lugged cartons out of the plane.

But he knew the answer to that. Take-off would be no problem, any more than it would for the other small transports at the far end of the strip.

These planes were not going to return, ever.

The work went on, and then it was done, or all but, and Chandler knew no more about it than when it was begun. The last little bit was a careful check of line voltages and balancing of biases. Chandler could help only up to a point, and then two execs, working through the bodies of one of the Hawaiians and the pilot of a Piper Tri-Pacer who had flown in some last-minute test equipment—and remained as part of the labor pool—laboriously worked on the final tests.

Spent, the other men flopped to the ground, waiting.

They were far gone. All of them, Chandler as much as the others. But one of them rolled over, grinned tightly at Chandler and said, "It's been fun. My name's Bradley. I always think people ought to know each other's names in cases like this—imagine sharing a grave with some utter stranger!"

"Grave?"

Bradley nodded. "Like Pharaoh's slaves. The pyramid is just about finished, friend. You don't know what I'm talking about?" He sat up, plucked the end of a tall blade of stemmy grass and put it between his teeth. "I guess you haven't seen the corpses in the woods."

Chandler said, "I found a town half a mile or so over there, nothing in it but skeletons."

"No, heavens, nothing that ancient. These are nice fresh corpses, out behind the junkheap there. Well, not *fresh*. They're a couple of weeks old. I thought it was neat of the Execs to dispose of the used-up labor out of sight of the rest of us. So much better for morale . . . until Juan Simoa and I went back looking for a plain, simple electrical extension cord and found them."

With icy calm Chandler realized that the man was talking sense. Used-up labor: the men who had unloaded the first planes, no doubt—worked until they dropped, then efficiently disposed of, as they were so cheap a commodity that they were not worth the trouble of hauling back to Honolulu for salvage. "I see," he said. "Besides, dead men tell no tales."

"*And* spread no disease. Probably that's why they did
their killing back in the tall trees. Always the chance some
exec might have to come down here to inspect in person.
Rotting corpses just aren't sanitary." Bradley grinned
again. "I used to be a doctor at Molokai."

"Lep—" began Chandler, but the doctor shook his
head.

"No, no, never say 'leprosy.' It's 'Hansen's disease.'
Whatever it is, the execs were sure scared of it. They wiped
out every patient we had, except a couple who got away
by swimming; then for good measure they wiped out most
of the medical staff, too, except for a couple like me who
were off-island and had the sense to keep quiet about
where they'd worked. Right down the beach it was."

Chandler said, "I was back in the village today. I
thought I saw someone still alive."

"You think it might be one of the lepers? It's possible.
But don't worry," said the doctor, rolling over on his back
and putting his hands behind his head. "Don't let a little
Hansen's disease scare you; we suffer from an infection far
worse than that." He yawned and said drowsily, "You
know, in the old days I used to work on pest-control for
the Public Health Service. We sure knocked off a lot of
rats and fleas. I never thought I'd be one of them...."

He was silent. Chandler looked at him more closely and
admired his courage very much. The man had fallen
asleep.

Chandler looked at the others. "You going to let them
kill us without a struggle?" he demanded.

The remaining Hawaiian was the only one to answer.
"Malihini," he said, "you just don't know how much
pilikia you're in. It isn't what we *let* them do."

"We'll see," Chandler promised grimly. "They're only
human. I haven't given up yet."

But in the end he could not save himself; it was the girl
who saved him.

That night Chandler tossed in troubled sleep, and woke

to find himself standing, walking toward the Tri-Pacer. The sun was just beginning to pink the sky and no one else was moving. "Sorry, love," he apologized to himself. "You probably need to bathe and shave, but I don't know how. Shave, I mean." He giggled. "Anyway, you'll find everything you need at my house."

He climbed into the plane. "Ever fly before?" he asked himself. "Well, you'll love it. Here we go—*close* the door . . . *snap* the belt . . . *turn* the switch." He admired the practiced ease with which his body started the motor, raced it with a critical eye on the instruments, turned the plane and lifted it off, up, into the rising sun.

"Oh, dear. You *do* need a bath," he told himself, wrinkling his nose humorously. "No harm. I've the nicest tub—pink, deep—and nine kinds of bath salts. But I wish you weren't so tired, love, because it's a long flight and you're wearing me out." He was silent as he bent to the correct compass heading and cranked a handle over his head to adjust the trim. "Koitska's going to be so *huhu*," he said, smiling. "Never fear, love, I can calm him down. But it's easier to do with you in one piece, you know, the other way's too late."

He was silent for a long time, and then his voice began to sing.

They were songs from Rosalie's own musical comedies. Even with so poor an instrument as Chandler's voice to work with, she sang well enough to keep both of them entertained while his body brought the plane in for a landing; and so Chandler went to live in the villa that belonged to Rosalie Pan.

XIV

"LOVE," SHE said, "there are worse things in the world than keeping me amused, when I'm not busy. We'll go to the beach again one day soon, I promise." And she was gone again.

It was like that every day.

Chandler was a concubine—not even that; he was a male geisha, convenient to play gin rummy with, or for company on the surfboards, or to make a drink.

He did not quite know what to make of himself. In bad times one hopes for survival. He had hoped; and now he had survival, perfumed and cushioned, but on what mad terms! Rosalie was a pretty girl, and a good-humored one. She was right. There were worse things in the world than being her companion; but Chandler could not adjust himself to the role.

It angered him when she got up from the garden swing and locked herself in her room—for he knew that she was not sleeping as she lay there, though her eyes were closed and she was motionless. It infuriated him when she casually usurped his body to bring an ashtray to her side, or to stop him when his hands presumed. And it drove him nearly wild to be a puppet with her friends working his strings.

He was that most of all. One exec who wished to communicate with another cast about for an available human proxy nearby. Chandler served for Rosie Pan: her telephone, her social secretary, and on occasion he was the garment her dates put on. For Rosalie was one of the few execs who cared to conduct any major part of her life in her own skin. She liked dancing. She enjoyed dining out. It was her pleasure to display herself to the worshippers at Luigi the Wharf Rat's and to speed down the long combers on a surfboard. When another exec chose to accompany her, it was Chandler's body which gave the remote "date" flesh.

He ate very well indeed—in surprising variety. He drank heavily sometimes and abstained others. Once, in the person of a Moroccan Exec, he smoked an opium pipe; once he dined on roasted puppy. He saw many interesting things and, when Rosalie was occupied without him, he had the run of her house, her music library, her pantry and her books. He was not mistreated. He was pampered and praised, and every night she kissed him before she retired to her own room with the snap-lock on the door.

He was miserable.

He prowled the house in the nights after she had left him, unable to sleep. It had been bad enough on Hilo, under the hanging threat of death. But then, though he was only a slave, he was working at something that used his skill and training.

Now? Now a Pekingese could do nearly all she wanted of him. He despised in himself the knowledge that with a Pekingese's cunning he was contriving to make himself indispensable to her—her slippers fetched in his teeth, his silky mane by her hand to stroke—if not these things in actuality, then their very near equivalents.

But what else was there for him?

There was nothing. She had spared his life from Koitska, and if he offended her Koitska's sentence would be carried out.

Even dying might be better than this, he thought.

Indeed, it might be better, even, to go back to Honolulu and life.

In the morning he woke to find himself climbing the wide, carpeted steps to her room. She was not asleep; it was her mind that was guiding him.

He opened the door. She lay with a feathery coverlet pulled up to her chin, eyes open, head propped on three pillows; as she looked at him he was free. "Something the matter, love? You fell asleep sitting up."

"Sorry."

She would not be put off. She made him tell her his resentments. She was very understanding and very sure as she said, "You're not a dog, love. I won't have you thinking that way. You're my friend. Don't you think I need a friend?" She leaned forward. Her nightgown was very sheer; but Chandler had tasted that trap before and he averted his eyes. "You think it's all fun for us. I understand. Tell me, if you thought I was doing important work—oh, *crucial* work, love—would you feel a little easier? Because I am. We've got the whole work of the island to do, and I do my share. We've got our plans to make and our future to provide for. There are so few of us. A single H-bomb could kill us all. Do you think it isn't work, keeping that bomb from ever coming here? There's all Honolulu to monitor, for they know about us there. We can't let some disgusting nitwits like your Society of Slaves destroy *us*. There's the problems of the world to see to. Why," she said with pride, "we've solved the whole Indian-Pakistani population problem in the last two months. They'll not have to worry about famine again for a dozen generations! We're working on China now; next Japan; next—oh, all the world. We'll have three-quarters of the lumps gone soon, and the rest will have space to breathe in. It's work!"

She saw his expression and said earnestly, "No, don't think that! You call it murder. It is, of course. But it's the surgeon's knife. We're quicker and less painful than starvation, love . . . and if some of us enjoy the work of weeding out the unfit, does that change anything? It does not! I admit some of us are, well, *mean*. But not all. And we're improving. The new people we take in are better than the old."

She looked at him thoughtfully for a moment.

Then she shook her head. "Never mind," she said— apparently to herself. "Forget it, love. Go like an angel and fetch us both some coffee."

Like an angel he went . . . not, he thought bitterly, like a man.

She was keeping something from him, and he was too stubborn to let her tease him out of his mood. "Everything's a secret," he complained, and she patted his cheek.

"It has to be that way." She was quite serious. "This is the biggest thing in the world. I'm fond of you, love, but I can't let that interfere with my duty."

"Shto, Rosie?" said Chandler's mouth thickly.

"Oh, there you are, Andrei," she said, and spoke quickly in Russian.

Chandler's brows knotted in a scowl and he barked: *"Nyeh mozhet bit!"*

"Andrei . . ." she said gently. *"Ya vas sprashniva-yoo . . ."*

"Nyet!"

"No Andrei . . ."

Rumble, grumble; Chandler's body twitched and fumed. He heard his own name in the argument, but what the subject matter was he could not tell. Rosalie was coaxing; Koitska was refusing. But he was weakening. After minutes Chandler's shoulders shrugged; he nodded; and he was free.

"Have some more coffee, love," said Rosalie Pan with an air of triumph.

Chandler waited. He did not understand what was going on. It was up to her to enlighten him, and finally she smiled and said: "Perhaps you can join us, love. Don't say yes or no. It isn't up to you . . . and besides you can't know whether you want it or not until you try. So be patient a moment."

Chandler frowned; then felt his body taken. His lips barked: *"Khorashaw!"* His body got up and walked to the wall of Rosalie's room. A picture on the wall moved aside and there was a safe. Flick, flick, Chandler's own fingers dialed a combination so rapidly that he could not follow it. The door of the safe opened.

And Chandler was free, and Rosalie excitedly leaping out of the bed behind him, careless of the wisp of nylon that was her only garment, crowding softly, warmly past him to reach inside the safe. She lifted out a coronet very like her own.

She paused and looked at Chandler.

"You can't do anything to harm us with this one, love," she warned. "Do you understand that? I mean, don't get the idea that you can tell anyone anything. Or do something violent. You can't. I'll be right with you, and Koitska will be monitoring the transmitter." She handed him the coronet. "Now, when you see something interesting, you move right in. You'll see how. It's the easiest thing in the world, and— Oh, here. Put it on."

Chandler swallowed with difficulty.

She was offering him the tool that had given the execs the world. A blunter, weaker tool than her own, no doubt. But still it was power beyond his imagining. He stood there frozen as she slipped it on his head. Sprung electrodes pressed gently against his temples and behind his ears. She touched something . . .

Chandler stood motionless for a moment and then, without effort, floated free of his own body.

Floating. Floating; a jellyfish floating. Trailing tentacles that whipped and curled, floating over the sandbound claws and chitin that clashed beneath, floating over the world's people, and them not even knowing, not even seeing . . .

Chandler floated.

He was up, out and away. He was drifting. Around him was no-color. He saw nothing of space or size, he only saw, or did not see but felt-smelled-tasted, people. They were the sandbound. They were the creatures that crawled and struggled below, and his tentacles lashed out at them.

Beside him floated another. The girl? It had a shape, but not a human shape—a cinctured area-rule shape. Female? Yes, undoubtedly the girl. It waved a member at him and he understood he was beckoned. He followed.

Two of the sandbound ones were ahead.

The female shape slipped into one, he into the other. It was as easy to invest this form with his own will as it was to order the muscles of his hand. They looked at each other out of sandbound eyes. "You're a boy!" Chandler laughed. The girl laughed: "You're an old washerwoman!" They were in a kitchen where fish simmered on an electric stove. The boy-Rosie wrinkled his-her nose, blinked and was empty. Only the small almond-eyed boy was left, and he began to cry convulsively. Chandler understood. He floated out after her.

This way, this way, she gestured. A crowd of mudbound figures. She slipped into one, he into another. They were in a bus now, rocking along an inland road, all men, all roughly dressed. Laborers going to clear a new section of Oahu of its split-level debris, Chandler thought, and looked for the girl in one of the men's eyes, could not find her, hesitated and—floated. She was hovering impatiently. This way!

He followed, and followed.

They were a hundred people doing a hundred things. They lingered a few moments as a teen-age couple holding hands in the twilight of the beach. They fled from a room where Chandler was an old woman dying on a bed, and Rosalie a stolid, uncaring nurse beside her. They played follow-the-leader through the audience of a Honolulu movie theater, and sought each other, laughing, among the fish stalls of King Street. Then Chandler turned to Rosalie to speak and . . . it all went out . . . the scene disappeared . . . he opened his eyes, and he was back in his own flesh.

He was lying on the pastel pile rug in Rosalie's bedroom.

He got up, rubbing the side of his face. He had tumbled, it seemed. Rosalie was lying on the bed. In a moment she opened her eyes.

"Well, love?"

He said hoarsely, "What made it stop?"

She shrugged. "Koitska turned you off. Tired of monitoring us, I expect—it's been an hour. I'm surprised his patience lasted this long."

She stretched luxuriously, but he was too full of what had happened even to see the white grace of her body. "Did you like it, love?" she asked. "Would you like to have it forever?"

XV

FOR NINE days Chandler's status remained in limbo. He spent those days in a state of numb detachment, remembering the men and women he had worn like garments, appalled and exhilarated.

He did not see Rosalie again that day. She kept to her room, and he was locked out.

He was still a lapdog.

But he was a lapdog with a dream dangling before him. He went to sleep that night thinking that he was a dog who might yet become a god, and had eight days left.

The next day Rosalie wheedled another hour of the coronet from Koitska. She and Chandler explored the ice caves on Mount Rainier, wearing the bodies of two sick and dying hermits they had found inhabiting a half-destroyed inn on its slopes. The mountain wore its cloudy flag of ice crystals in a bleak, pale evening. The air was thin and stinging, and their borrowed bodies ached. They left them and found two others, twenty-five hundred miles to the east, and wandered arm in arm under stars, neared the destroyed International Bridge at Niagara, breathing the spray of the unchanging Falls. They came back in a flash when Koitska's patience ran out again and sprawled on her hot, dry lawn, and he had seven days left.

They passed like a dream.

Chandler saw a great deal of the inner workings of the Exec. He had privileges, for he was up for membership in the club. Rosalie had proposed him.

He talked with two Czechoslovakian ballet dancers in their persons—lean, dark girls who laughed and frowned alternately—and with a succession of heavily accented Russians and Poles and Japanese, who came to him only through the mouth of the beach boy-servant who worked on Rosalie's garden. Chandler thought they liked him. He was pleased that he had penetrated where he had not been allowed before . . . until he realized that these freedoms were in themselves a threat.

They allowed him this contact for a reason. They were looking him over.

If their final decision was to reject him, as it well might be, they would have to kill him, because he had seen too much.

But he had little time to dwell on fears of the future. The present was crowded. On the fourth day one of the members of the exec invited him to join them.

"You'll do for a gang boss, Shanda-lerra," he said through the beach boy's mouth; and once again Chandler found himself working on an executive committee project, though no one had told him what it was. He swam up into the strange, thin sea of the mind, in company with a dozen others, and they arrowed through emptiness to a place Chandler could not recognize. He watched the others spiral down and slip into the bodies of the tiny mud-dwelling dolls that were human beings. When they were all gone he sought a doll-body of his own.

He opened his eyes on a bleak, snow-laden Arctic dawn.

A shrieking blast from the North Pole was driving particles of gritty ice into his eyes, his ears, the loose, quilted clothes his body wore. The temperature, he was sure, was far below zero. The cold made his teeth ache, filled his eyes with tears.

All around him great floodlights mounted on poles cast a harsh glare over a hundred acres of barren earth, studded with sheds and concrete pillboxes, heaped over with dirt and snow. In the center of the great lighted ice-desert loomed a skeletal steel object that looked like a madly displaced skyscraper.

It rose hundreds of feet into the air, its top beyond the range of the floodlights, its base fogged by driving snow. Chandler looked again; no, it was not a single skyscraper but two of them, two tall steel towers, one like an elongated projectile standing on its tail, the other like the Eiffel Tower, torn out of context.

Someone caught Chandler's arm and bellowed hoarsely: "Come on, darling! That is you, isn't it? Come over here where Djelenko's handing out the guns."

He recognized Rosalie, clad in the corpus of a Siberian yak-herder, and followed her docilely toward a man who was unlocking a concrete bunker. It was not only the girl he had recognized. With an active shock of surprise he saw that the twin towers were a rocket and its gantry. By the size of it, an orbital rocket at the least.

"I didn't think there were any satellites left!" he bellowed into the flat, dirty ear that was at present the property of Rosalie Pan.

The broad, dark-browed face turned toward him. "This'un's about the last, I guess," she shouted. "Wouldn't be out in this mess otherwise! Miserable weather, ain't it?" She pushed him toward the bunker. "Go see Djelenko, love! Faster we get to work, faster we get this over with."

But Djelenko was shouting something at them that Chandler could not understand.

"Oh, damn," cried Rosalie. "Love, you went and got yourself the wrong body. This chap's one of the old experts. Zip out of it and pick yourself a nice Mongol like mine."

Confused, Chandler brought his body's fist up before his eyes. The hand was calloused, scarred and twisted with cold—and one finger, its nail mashed, was trying its best to hurt in the numbing chill of the Siberian air—but the fingers had started out to be long and white. They were not the blunt fists of the yak-herders.

"Sorry," shouted Chandler, and took himself out of the body.

What price the Orphalese? What price the murder of so many innocents, including his own wife? For them, and all of them, Chandler did not have a thought. This was his tryout at the spring training of the team, his first day on the new job. Conscientiously he was attempting to acquire the knack of being a demon.

If he regretted anything at this moment, it was only his own lack of expertise. He wished he were a better demon than he was. He hung irresolute in the queerness of this luminous, distorted sea. He saw the sand-dweller he had just quit, moving in its shapeless way toward the place where he knew the gantries stood. There were others like it about—but which should he enter? He swore to himself. No doubt there were recognition marks that were easy enough to find; neither Rosalie nor the other members of the Exec seemed to have much difficulty making their way about. But he lacked pieces for the puzzle, and he was confused.

He reasoned the pattern out: The gantries meant a rocket flight. The European body he had tenanted for a moment was not native to the region: a slave expert, no doubt, once perhaps an official on this project and now impressed into the service of the executive committee. No doubt the Mongols were mere warm bodies, casually commandeered from their nearby villages, to be used for haul-and-lift labor as need be.

Probably the largest groups of doll-bodies would be the Mongols; so he selected one at random, entered it and stood up again into the noise and pain of the freezing gale.

He had a pick in his hand. There were forty or fifty like him in this work crew, digging with antlike tenacity—and antlike results—into the flinty, frozen ground. Apparently they were trying to set stakes to help moor the gantries against the gale.

He dropped the pick and rubbed numbed fingers together. He realized at once that he had not chosen a very good body. For one thing, it had a squint which made everything look fuzzy and doubled; until he learned to adjust to it he was almost blind. For another, it ached with the effects of a very long time of forced labor and hunger. And it was lousy.

Well, he thought, I can stand anything for a while. Let's get to work. . . . And then he saw that a body very like his own—but a body which was inhabited by a member of the Exec, since it was carrying a rifle—gestured to him, screaming something he could not understand.

He doesn't know I am me, thought Chandler, half amused. He started toward the rifleman. "Wait a minute," he called. "I'm Chandler. I'm ready to go to work, if you'll just tell me what to—hey! Wait!"

He was very surprised to see that the rifleman was not even making an attempt to understand him. The figure raised its rifle, pointed it at him and fired. That was all.

Chandler was very seriously annoyed. It was a clear, careless matter of mistaken identity, he thought angrily. How stupid of the man!

He felt the first shock of the bullet entering his body but did not wait for more. He did not linger to taste death, or even pain. Before either could reach his mind he was up and out of the body again, fuming and mad. Stupid! he thought. Somebody ought to get called down for this!

A dizzying sense of falling. A soundless explosion of light.

Then he was back in a body: his own.

He picked himself up and stood looking out of Rosalie Pan's picture window onto the thin green lawn, still angry. He had been turned off. Somehow Koitska, or whatever other member of the executive committee had been watching over him, had observed his blundering. His relay coronet had been turned off, and he was back in Hawaii.

Well, he thought grudgingly, that part was all right. He probably was better off out of the way—at least, if they didn't have sense enough to brief him ahead of time. But the rest of the affair was plain stupidity! He had been frozen, scared and pushed about for nothing!

He rubbed his ear angrily. It was soft and warm, not the chilled, numbed thing he had worn moments before. He muttered imprecations at the damned foolishness of the executive committee. If he couldn't run things better than they, he told himself, he would just give up. . . .

Ten or fifteen minutes later it occurred to him that he had not, after all, been the greatest loser from that particular blunder.

A few minutes later still something else occurred to him. He was not merely beginning to live the life of the execs; he was beginning to think like them, too.

An hour later Rosalie came lightly down the stairs, yawning and stretching. "Love," she cried, catching sight of Chandler, "you really screwed that one up. Can't you tell a Kraut missile expert from a Mongolian cowboy?"

Chandler said glumly, "No."

She said consolingly, but with a touch of annoyance, too, "Oh, don't be frightful, love. I know it was a disappointment, but—"

"It must've disappointed the man I got killed, too," said Chandler.

"You *are* being frightful. Well, I understand." She patted his arm. "It's the waiting. It's so nervous-making. Embarrassing, too."

"How would you know?"

"Why, love," she said, "don't you think I went through it myself? But it passes, dear, it passes. Meanwhile come have a drink."

Moodily Chandler allowed the girl to soothe him, although he thought she was taking far too light a view of it. He accepted the Scotch from her and tasted it without comment.

"Is something wrong with it, love?"

He said patiently, "You know I don't like too much water in a drink."

"I'm sorry, love."

He shrugged.

Well, he thought, she was right. In a way. He was indeed being frightful. He did not see why she would respond with annoyance, however. He had a right to act a little odd, when he was, after all, betraying all of his friends, even the memory of his dead wife. She certainly could not expect him to take all of that in his stride, without a moment's regret.

Rosalie yawned and smothered it. "I'm sorry, love. Funny how it tires you out to work in somebody else's body!"

"Yes."

"Oh, really, now!" she was angry at last. "For cat's sake, love! Mooning around like a puppy that's been swatted for making a mess!"

He said, "I'm sorry if I have been in any way annoying to—"

"Come off it! This is Rosie you're talking to." She cradled his head in her arm like a mother—an irritated mother, but a mother. " 'Smatter? Are you scared?"

He put down the Scotch and admitted, "A little bit. I think so."

"Well, why didn't you say so? Dear heart, everybody's scared waiting for the votes to come in. Very nervous-making waiting to know."

He demanded, "When will I know?"

She hesitated. "I'm not supposed to discuss some things with you, love, you know that. Not yet."

"When Rosie?"

She capitulated. "Well, I don't suppose it makes much difference under the circumstances—"

He knew what circumstances she meant.

"—so I'll tell you that much, anyway. See, love, you need a little over seven hundred votes to get in. That's a lot, isn't it? But that's the rules of the game. And right now you have, let's see—"

Her eyes glazed for a moment. Chandler knew that she was looking out at something else, through some clerk's vision somewhere on the island—or somewhere in the world.

"Right now you have about a hundred and fifty. Takes time, doesn't it?"

"That's a hundred and fifty to let me in, right? And how many 'no' votes?"

She patted his hand and said gently, "None of those, love. You wouldn't ever have but one." She got up and refilled his drink. "Never fear, dear," she said. "Rosie's on your side! And now let's have something to eat, eh?"

And he had seven days left.

XVI

TIME PASSED. Chandler wheedled information out of Rosalie until he had a clear picture of what he was up against. Two-thirds of all the members of the executive committee had to cast an affirmative vote for him (but they would vote in blocs, Rosalie promised; get this one on his side and she would bring in fifty more, get that one and he could deliver a hundred). If there were a single blackball he was out. And he had ten days to be accepted, which were going fast.

Very fast. He had no idea that so many things could be done so rapidly. He was meeting people by the dozen and score, members of the Exec who were Rosalie's personal friends, all of them votes if he could please them. He did everything he could think of to please them. He was working, too—not on the rocket project any more; and not on any of the other off-Island projects of the exec (which was all right with him, as he felt pretty sure that most of these involved selective murder and demolition); but on little odds and ends of electronic jobs for Koitska and others. He was allowed to go into Honolulu for more parts, which the new owner of Parts 'n Plenty provided for him in silence. Her eyes were red with weeping; she was Hsi's widow. Chandler tried to find something to say to her, ran through every possible word in his vocabulary, and left without speaking at all.

Chandler knew that his very great measure of freedom was a dangerous sign. Koitska did not trouble to hide

from him any more just what it was that they had built on
Hilo. He even allowed Chandler to do some patch-cording
and soldering on the installation in the former TWA Message Center—watching him every minute, gasping and
snoring as he lay on his couch across the room—and
made no effort to keep Chandler from guessing that the
Hilo assembly was almost a duplicate of the one here. Hilo
had more power, Chandler thought; there had been some
hint that more power was needed for the really remote
control applications involved in the Executive Committee's
Mars project; but basically it was only a standby.
Checking current flows under Koitska's eye, Chandler
thought detachedly that it might just be possible, if one
were both daring and very lucky, to overcome the Exec,
destroy the installation, find a way to Hilo and destroy that
one too.... One did not take that sort of risk lightly, of
course, he acknowledged. It was an easy way to get killed.

And he did not want to get killed.

He wanted to live very much ... as a member in good
standing of the Executive Committee.

The Russian POWs who manned Hitler's Atlantic Wall
would have understood Chandler's reasoning; so would
the Americans who broadcast for the enemy in Korea. The
ultimately important thing for any man was to stay alive.

Chandler had not forgotten Peggy Flershem or the
Orphalese, or Hsi and his tortured friends around the
Monument. He merely thought, quite reasonably, that he
could do nothing to help them any more; and meanwhile
he had to pick up several hundred more votes or he would
join them all in death. He acknowledged that it was in
some sense degrading that, chances were, the men and
women he curried favor with today were perhaps the very
ones who had shot Ellen Braisted in Orphalese, raped and
murdered his wife through the person of his friend, Jack
Souther, kidnaped the children who had flown across the
Pacific with him ... there was no sense in cataloguing all
the possible abominations these men and women had
committed, he told himself firmly. All that was as dead as
Hsi.

Life was important. On any terms, life.

Considered objectively, the Orphalese and the people in his own home town who had been destroyed by the execs were of no more importance than the stolid, half-frozen Siberians whom he had actually helped (even if ineffectually!) to work to death. Or the inhabitants of the destroyed village in Hilo. Or the peaceful people of New York when the submarine exploded itself in the harbor. Or. . . .

He sighed. It was very difficult to stop making catalogues, or to turn from that to a friendly smile and a gay, friendship-winning quip.

But he managed the task. It revolted him, said Pooh-Bah. But he did it.

When she could Rosalie borrowed the use of a coronet for him and they roamed the world, to night clubs in Juarez and lamaseries under the Himalayan peaks, to every place that she thought might amuse and divert him. On the fourth day she took him to a very special place indeed. "You'll like it," was all she would say. "Oh! I haven't been there for months."

It was half a world away. Chandler had never learned to read the topologically insane patterns of grayed light but he knew it was very distant, and it turned out in fact to be in Italy. They found bodies to wear and commandeered a boat and headed out over blue water, Rosalie claiming she knew where she was going. But when, after repeated sightings on the coast behind them, she cut the little electric motor, the water in which they drifted looked like any other water to Chandler. "I hope you know what you're doing," he said.

"Of course, love! And I adore your mustachios."

He preened them. He rather fancied the body he had found, too; it had come with a gun and a plumed hat, but he had discarded them on the beach where they found the boat. Rosalie had done herself well enough, in a costume of flesh that was not more than eighteen years old, not taller than five feet one and darkly beautiful. She stood up, rocking the boat. "Everybody in the water!" she called. "Last one in's a malihini!"

"Swimming? Swimming where?" he demanded. She was already taking off her clothes, the ruffled shirt, the toreador pants; in brief underwear she climbed to the gunwale and tugged at his mustache.

"Straight down, love. You'll like it."

He stood up and began taking off the coat and the uniform pants with their broad stripe of gold. "Wait a minute," he grumbled. "It always takes longer for a man to get his clothes off. He doesn't get as much practice, I suppose."

"Love! You're terribly anti-woman! Follow me!" And she dived from the gunwale, neat and clean, heading down.

Chandler followed. He had never been a great swimmer and was, in fact, not very fond of water sports. You can't get hurt, he reminded himself as he swam down into the dark after the pale, wriggling shape that was Rosalie's body. But it *felt* as if he could get hurt. He was ten yards down, and fifteen, and the end not in sight; and he could feel his borrowed heart pounding and the carabinieri's lungs craving to breathe. The warm Adriatic water was clouded and dim. He could see nothing except for Rosalie, down below—no. There was something else, he could not be sure what. Something darker, and square in outline. . . .

Rosalie's slim, pale form slipped under it and disappeared.

Grimly Chandler followed, his muscles tiring, his lungs bursting. With the last of his strength he skirted the dark square thing and came up beneath it. It was a thirty-foot rectangle of metal, he could see now, pierced with darkened windows, swinging on long chains that stretched downward into invisibility.

Where Rosalie had gone there was a square of a different color. It looked like a hatch.

It was a hatch. He bobbed up through it and into a dark bubble of air, puffing and gasping.

Rosalie was there before him, sprawled out of the water onto the metal deck, wheezing like himself. "Whew, love," she panted. "Come on up. You've done the hard part. Now let's see if I can find the lights."

The lights were tiny lanterns for which Rosalie found flashlight cells somewhere. They illuminated a chamber containing tables, chairs, beds, racks of instruments, cupboards of food.

"Isn't it nice, love? Wasn't I lucky to find it?"

Chandler stared about, beginning to breathe normally again. "What is it?"

"Some sort of experiment, I think." She had found a mirror, coated with grime and was scrubbing it clean with someone's neatly folded sweatshirt. "People used to live here in the old days," she said, propping the mirror against a wall and pirouetting in front of it. "Oh, lovely! Really I looked a little bit like this once, back in—well!"

"Now what do we do?"

She pressed her hair back, squeezing water out of it. "Why, we rest for a minute, love. And if I can find it, we drink some champagne. And then we do something very nice."

Chandler picked up a harpoon gun and put it down again. He could not help wondering who had built this trapped bubble of underwater living-space. "Cousteau," he said out loud, remembering.

"You mean that skin-diver? Well, no, I don't think so, love. He was French. But it's the same idea." She produced a bottle from a chest. "Champagne!" she crowed. "Just as I promised. A bit warm, I'm afraid, but still it'll give you heart for the next bit."

"And what's that?"

But she would not tell him, only fussed over him while he popped the scarlet plastic cork out with his thumbs and retreated, laughing, from the gush of foam.

They drank, out of a mug and a canteen cup. Chandler could not help prodding at her for information. "The boat's going to be drifted away, you know. How do we get back?"

"Oh, love, you do worry about the most peculiar things. I do wish you'd relax."

"It's not entirely easy—" he began, but she flared at him.

"Oh, come on! I must say, you've got a pretty—" But she relented almost at once. "I'm sorry for snapping at you. I know it's a scary time." She sat down beside him, her bare arm touching his, and said, "We might as well finish the champagne before we go. Want me to tell you about when I went through it?"

"Sure," he said, stirring the wine around in the glass and drinking it down, hardly hearing what she said, although the sound of her voice was welcome.

"Oh, that lousy headdress! It weighed twenty pounds, and they put it on with hatpins." He caressed her absently. He had figured out that she was talking about the night New York was bombed. "I was in the middle of the big first-act curtain number when—" her face was strained, even after years, even now that she was herself one of the godlike ones—"when something took hold of me. I ran off the stage and right out through the front door. There was a cab waiting. As soon as I got in I was free, and the driver took off like a lunatic through the tunnel, out to Newark Airport. I tell you, I was scared! At the toll-booth I screamed but my—friend—let go of the driver for a minute, smashed a trailer-truck into a police car, and in the confusion we got away. He took me over again at the airport. I ran bare as a bird into a plane that was just ready to take off. The pilot was under control. . . . We flew eleven hours, and I wore that damn feather headdress all the way."

She held out her glass for a refill. Chandler busied himself opening the second bottle. Now she was talking about her friend. "I hadn't seen him in six years. I was just a kid, living in Islip. He was with a Russian trade commission next door, in an old mansion. Well, he was one of the ones, back in Russia, that came up with these." She touched her brow where her coronet usually rested. "So," she said brightly, "he put me up for membership and by and by they gave me one. You see? It's all very simple, except the waiting."

Chandler pulled her to him and made a toast. "Your friend."

"He's a nice guy," she said moodily, sipping her drink. "You know how careful I am about getting exercise and so on? It's partly because of him. You would have liked him, love, only—well, it turned out that he liked me well enough, but he began to like what he could get through the coronet a lot more. He got fat. A lot of them are awfully fat, love," she said seriously. "That's why they need people like me. And you. Replacements. Heart trouble, liver trouble, what can they expect when they lie in bed day in and day out, taking their lives through other people's bodies? I won't let myself go that way. . . . It's a temptation. You know, almost every day I find some poor woman on a diet and spend a solid hour eating cream-puffs and gravies. How they must hate me!"

She grinned, leaned back and kissed him.

Chandler put his arms around the girl and returned the kiss, hard. She did not draw away. She clung to him, and he could feel in the warmth of her body, the sound of her breath that she was responding.

And then she whispered, "Not yet, love," and pushed him away. "Time for water sports!" she cried, getting to her feet. "You've loafed here long enough—now let me show you what's *fun!*"

Ten minutes later, wearing scuba gear Rosalie had turned up from somewhere, he was following her out through the grayish green sea.

After the first minute, it was not like swimming at all. For one thing, you didn't feel wet. And you were breathing, through the mask and the tube in your teeth. It was interesting, he thought; but he could not help wondering if this was what Rosalie had meant by "fun."

They had weighted themselves with belts of metal slugs, but he was still buoyant and had to fight continually against rising to the surface, where Rosalie seemed to have overweighted herself and kept sloping down toward the distant bottom. Swimming was slow, especially as Rosalie had insisted he carry a long-bladed butcher knife—"In case of sharks, love!"

But still! He was under the water and breathing. He followed her, expecting something, but not knowing quite what.

There were sharks, all right. He had seen a dozen of them, and there was something off to the side right now, circling behind him, almost invisible in the distance. He regarded it with great suspicion and dislike. Even if you couldn't get really killed in a borrowed body—you yourself couldn't; he was not prepared to think about what happened to the prisoned owner of the body—there were things that were not attractive about the prospect of great unseen jaws suddenly slicing a ham away.

Rosalie half turned to him, beckoned and started down. Dimly he could see the bottom now, or at any rate something that was where the bottom ought to be. Rosalie was spinning there below him, waiting for him.

It was quite dim, this far from the surface of the sea, but Chandler could see the gleam of her eye and her cheerful wink behind the mask. She stretched out a hand and pointed above him and behind.

Chandler half turned to see. There were five of the great shadowy bulks there now, and they seemed to be moving toward him.

Frantically he kicked and squirmed to face them, but Rosalie caught his arm. She held him, and gestured for him to hand her the knife.

Chandler was frankly terrified. Every childhood fear sprang to life in him; his breath caught, his heart pounded, something churned in his belly and forced its way into his throat. It was no good telling himself that this was not really his body, that his own flesh lay secure in a split-level living room twelve thousand miles away; he cringed from the threat of the grim, silent shapes and it was all he could do to stay in this threatened corpus to see what Rosalie wanted to do.

He gave her the knife. She glanced upward at the sharks calculatingly, then pursed her lips, winked, blew him a kiss and neatly, carefully, sliced his airhose in two.

His oxygen blew out in a cascade of great, wriggling bubbles. Water rushed in. He felt her tearing his facemask off, but water was already in his eyes, mouth, nose. He coughed and strangled, more startled than he had ever been in his life; and then she touched his chest with the blade, daintily and precisely. Fire leaped along his side and a cloud of blood began to diffuse through the water.

She ripped off her own facemask and slit a careful line across the eighteen-year-old's borrowed abdomen, then reached out her arms to him.

They kissed. Her arms locked around him like manacles.

He felt his lungs bursting as they kissed and spun, thrashing, through the water, while the feathery clouds of blood spread out; and as they turned Chandler saw the great torpedo shapes, now incredibly close, coming toward them incredibly fast.

The last he saw was the great yawning grin of teeth; and then he could not help it, he fled. He abandoned Rosalie, abandoned the borrowed body of the carabinieri, fled and did not stop until he was back in his own flesh, still frightened, and violently ill.

XVII

CHANDLER COULD sleep only tardily that night, and not well. His sleep was punctuated with sudden wakenings, illuminated with dreams. Ellen Braisted came and spoke to him, and Margot his wife. They did not threaten or terrify him. They only looked at him with reproach ... and when he woke and it was broad daylight, and the Kanaka was whirring the lawnmower across the grass outside just as though no murders had been committed by the inmates of the house, he slouched angrily around the living room for an hour and then began to drink.

By the time Rosalie Pan came downstairs, yawning and looking slaked and contented, he was drunk enough to coax her into breakfasting on Bloody Marys.

By the time she had had her third, and no longer minded the fact that she had not eaten, Chandler was stumbling and stammering. Rosalie did not object. Perhaps she understood, or understood at least that she had shown him something of herself that took getting used to. Even when the other members of the exec began calling in, usually through the person of the beach boy who was her handyman, she laughed and made excuses for Chandler. But when they were gone—when it was only the Kanaka who was in the room with them, turning to leave with a tired fear—she reproached him gently: "Not quite so much of the arm-around-the-neck, love. Do you mind? I mean, everything in its place."

"You didn't mind yesterday," said Chandler sullenly.

"Oh, really! I'm not trying to reform you, you know. But these are members of the exec, and you need their votes."

"I certainly wouldn't want to behave badly in the presence of a member of the exec," said Chandler, and lurched to the kitchen for another bottle. He was at that stage of drunkenness when he felt he was not going to be able to get drunk: he observed the symptoms of hands and feet and mouth, and cursed the clarity of his brain that would not anesthetize him. In the kitchen he paused, staggered over to the sink and on impulse put his head under the cold-water tap.

When Rosalie came looking for him minutes later she

found him brewing coffee. "Why, that's *better*, love," she cried. "I thought you were going to drink the island dry!"

He poured a cup of the stuff, hot and black, and began to swallow it in small, painful gulps. Rosalie fetched a cup for herself, added cream and sugar and sat at the table. "Time's wasting," she said practically, "and you don't have the votes yet, love. I want you to work on Koitska today. Tell him all about the geraniums and what-you-call-thems; he can bring you fifty votes if he wants to."

Chandler finished the coffee and poured another cup. This time he added a generous shot of whiskey to it. Rosalie tightened her lips, but only said, "Then there's that bunch from the East Coast, the Embassy girls and Brad and Tony. They've already voted, but they could get out some more for you if you got them interested. Brad's been a doll, but the girls have all sorts of friends they haven't done anything with."

Chandler lit a cigarette and let her talk. He knew it was important to him. He knew she was trying to help him, and indeed that without her help he was a dead man. He simply could not bring himself to play up to her mood. He stood up and said, "I'm going to take a bath." And he left her sitting there.

And ten minutes later he came shouting into her room, his body still wet from the shower, wearing a pair of khaki shorts and nothing else. "Who?" he cried. "Who did you say? What's the name of your friend?"

Rosalie, sitting at her vanity mirror, wearing nothing but underwear and her coronet, took her hands away from her hair and looked at him. "Love! What's the matter?"

"Answer me, damn it! Brad! Brad who?"

She said, with little patience, "Do you mean Brad Fe-nell? I must say, the way you're acting I don't know why he should go out of his way— What's the matter?"

Chandler's eyes were glaring and he had begun to shake. He sat down limply on her bed, staring at her.

"You mean Brad Fenell is helping me? If I get elected to the exec, it will be because of Brad Fenell?"

"Well, love, I have a little something to do with it, too. But Brad's been lovely."

Chandler nodded. "Lovely," he said faintly. "A real doll."

"You remember him, don't you? At the party night before last? The little dark fellow?"

"I remember him." And he did; but he hadn't, there for a while. He hadn't remembered at all what Ellen Braisted had told him. The Brad Fenell who had debased and tortured her, who had finally murdered her, was now a powerful friend. There was a joke about that, mused Chandler. With that sort of friend, you didn't need any enemy.

But on all the Executive Committee, what other sort of friend could there possibly be?

Rosalie's irritation was lost in alarm now. Something was clearly wrong with Chandler. She was in very little doubt what it was; she knew nothing of Ellen Braisted, but she knew enough of the exec in general, herself included, to have a shrewd notion of what personal nerve had somehow been touched, and she came over and sat beside him. "Love," she said gently, "It's not as bad as you think. There are good things, too."

Chandler said unrelentingly, "Name one."

"Oh, love! Don't be awful." She put her arm around him. "It's just another few days," she soothed, "and then you can do what you like. Isn't that worth it? I mean *really* what you like, love. A whole world to play in. . . ."

Get thee behind me, thought Chandler numbly. But she was right. It was too bad, but facts were facts, he told himself reasonably. Good-by, Ellen, he thought. Good-by, Margot. And he turned to the girl beside him. . . .

And stiffened and felt himself seized.

"Vi myenya zvali?" his own voice demanded, harsh and mocking.

The girl tried to push him away. Her eyes were bright and huge, staring at him. "Andrei!"

"Da, Andrei! Kok eto dosadno!"

"Andrei, please. I know you're—"

"Filthy!" screamed Chandler's voice. "How can you? I do not allow this carrion to touch you so—not vot is mine —I do not allow him to live!" And Chandler dropped her and leaped to his feet.

He fought. He struggled; but only in his mind, and helplessly; his body carried him out of the room in spite of his struggles, running and stumbling, out into the drive, into her waiting car and away.

He drove like a madman on roads he had never seen before. The car's gears bellowed pain at their abuse, the tires screamed.

Chandler, imprisoned inside himself, recognized that touch. Koitska! He knew who Rosalie Pan's lover had been. If he had been in doubt his own voice, raucous and hysterical with rage, told him the truth. All that long drive it screamed threats and obscenities at him, in Russian and tortured English.

The car stopped in front of the TWA facility and, still imprisoned, his body hurried in, bruising itself deliberately against every doorpost and stick of furniture. "I could have smashed you in the car!" his voice screamed hoarsely. "It is too merciful. I could have thrown you into the sea! It is not painful enough."

In the garage his body stopped and looked wildly around. "Knives, torches," his lips chanted. "Shall I gouge out eyes? Slit throat?"

A jar of battery acid stood on a shelf. *"Da, da!"* screamed Chandler, stumbling toward it. "One drink, eh? And I von't even stay vith you to feel it, the pain—just a moment—then it eats the guts, the long slow dying. . ." And all the time the body that was Chandler's was clawing the cap off the jar, tilting it—

He dropped the jar, and leaped aside instinctively as it splintered at his feet.

He was free!

Before he could move he was seized again, stumbled, crashed into a wall—

And was free again.

He stood waiting for a moment, unable to believe it; but he was still free. The alien invader did not seize his mind. There was no sound. No one moved. No gun fired at him, no danger threatened.

He *was* free; he took a step, turned, shook his head and proved it.

He was free and, in a moment, realized that he was in the building with the fat bloated body of the man who wanted to murder him, the body that in its own strength could scarcely stand erect.

It was suicide to attempt to harm an exec. He would certainly lose his life—except—that was gone already anyhow; he had lost it. He had nothing left to lose.

XVIII

CHANDLER LOPED silently up the stairs to Koitska's suite.

Halfway up he tripped and sprawled, half stunning himself against the stair rail. It had not been his own clumsiness, he was sure. Koitska had caught at his mind again. But only feebly. Chandler did not wait. Whatever was interfering with Koitska's control, some distraction or malfunction of the coronet or whatever, Chandler could not bank on its lasting.

The door was locked.

He found a heavy mahogany chair, with a back of solid carved wood. He flung it onto his shoulders, grunting, and ran with it into the door, a bull driven frantic, lunging out of its querencia to batter the wall of the arena. The door splintered.

Chandler was gashed with long slivers of wood, but he was through the door.

Koitska lay sprawled along his couch, eyes staring.

Alive or dead? Chandler did not wait to find out but sprang at him with hands outstretched. The staring eyes flickered; Chandler felt the pull at his mind. But Koitska's strength was almost gone. The eyes glazed, and Chandler was upon him. He ripped the coronet off and flung it aside, and the huge bulk of Koitska swung paralytically off the couch and fell to the floor.

The man was helpless. He lay breathing like a steam engine, one eye pressed shut against the leg of a coffee table, the other looking up at Chandler.

Chandler was panting almost as hard as the helpless mass at his feet. He was safe for a moment. At the most for a moment, for at any time one of the other execs might dart down out of the mind-world into the real, looking at the scene through Chandler's eyes and surely deducing what would be even less to his favor than the truth. He had to get away from there. If he seemed busy in another room perhaps they would go away again. Chandler turned his back on the paralyzed monster to flee. It would be even better to try to lose himself in Honolulu—if he could get that far—he did not in his own flesh know how to fly the helicopter that was parked in the yard or he would try to get farther still.

But as he turned he was caught.

Chandler's body turned to see Koitska lying there, and screamed.

His eyes were staring at Koitska. It was too late. He was possessed by someone, he did not know whom. Though it made little enough difference, he thought, watching his own hands reach out to touch the staring face.

His body straightened, his eyes looked around the room, he went to the desk. "Love," he cried to himself, "what's the matter with Koitska? Write, for God's sake!" And he took a pencil in his hand and was free.

He hesitated, then scribbled: *I don't know. I think he had a stroke. Who are you?*

The other mind slipped tentatively into his, scanning the paper. "Rosie, you idiot, who did you think?" he said furiously. "What have you done?"

Nothing, he began instinctively, then scratched the word out. Briskly and exactly he wrote: *He was going to kill me, but he had some kind of an attack. I took his coronet away. I was going to run.*

"Oh, you fool," he told himself shrilly a moment later. Chandler's body knelt beside the wheezing fat lump, taking its pulse. The faint, fitful throb meant nothing to Chandler; probably meant nothing to Rosie either, for his body stood up, hesitated, shook its head. "You've done it now," he sobbed, and was surprised to find he was weeping real tears. "Oh, love, why? I could have taken care of Koitska—somehow— No, maybe I couldn't," he said frantically, breaking down. "I don't know what to do. Do you have any ideas—outside of running?"

It took him several seconds to write the one word, but it was really all he could find to write. *No.*

His lips twisted as his eyes read the word. "Well," he said practically, "I guess that's the end, love. I mean, I give up."

He got up, turned around the room. "I don't know," he told himself worriedly. "There might be a chance—if we could hush this up. I'd better get a doctor. He'll have to use your body, so don't be surprised if there's someone and it isn't me. Maybe he can pull Andrei through. Maybe Andrei'll forgive you then— Or if he dies," Chandler's voice schemed as his eyes stared at the rasping motionless hulk, "we can say you broke down the door to *help* him. Only you'll have to put his coronet back on, so it won't look suspicious. Besides that will keep anyone from occupying him. Do that, love. Hurry." And he was free.

Gingerly Chandler crossed the floor.

He did not like to touch the dying animal that wheezed

before him, liked even less to give it back the weapon that, if it had as much as five minutes of sentience again, it would use to kill him. But the girl was right. Without the helmet any wandering curious exec might possess Koitska himself. The helmet would shield him from—

Would shield anyone from—

Would shield even Chandler himself from possession if he used it!

He did not hesitate. He slipped the helmet on his head, snapped the switch and in a moment stood free of his own body, in the gray, luminous limbo, looking down at the pallid traceries that lay beneath.

He did not pause to think or plan; it was as though he had planned every step, in long detail, over many years. Chandler for at least a few moments had the freedom to battle the execs on their own ground, the freedom that any mourning parent or husband in the outside world would know well how to use.

Chandler also knew how. He was a weapon.

The coronet that he wore now was no limited, monitored slave device; it was Koitska's own. While he wore it Chandler could not be touched.

Perhaps it was the aftermath of these wearing, terrifying days; perhaps it was the residual poison of his morning of drinking and night of little sleep. Chandler felt both placid and prepared. There would be a way to use this weapon against the Exec, and he would find it. Margot, Ellen Braisted, Meggie, Hsi—a billion others—all would be revenged. He would very likely die for it, but he was a dead man anyway.

In any case it was not a great thing to die; millions had done it for nothing under the rule of the execs, and he was privileged to be able to die trying to kill *them*.

He stepped callously around the hulk on the floor and found a door behind the couch, a door and a hall, and at the end of that hall a large room that had once perhaps been a message center. Now it held rack after rack of electronic gear. He recognized it without elation.

It was the main transmitter for all the coronets of the exec.

He had only to pull one switch—that one there—and power would cease to flow. The coronets would be dead. The execs would be only human beings again. In five minutes he could destroy enough parts that it would be at least a week's work to build it again, and in a week the slaves in Honolulu—somehow he could reach them, somehow he would tell them of their chance—could root out and destroy every exec on all the islands.

Of course, there was the standby transmitter he himself had helped to build.

He realized tardily that Koitska would have made some arrangement for starting that up by remote control.

He put down the tool-kit with which he had been advancing on the racks of transistors, and paused to think.

He was a fool, he saw after a moment. He could not destroy this installation—not yet—not until he had used it. He remembered to sit down so that his body would not crash to the floor, and then he sent himself out and up, to scan the nearby area.

There was no one there, nobody within a mile or more, except the feeble glimmer that was dying Koitska. He did not enter that body. He returned to his own long enough to lock the door, and then he went up and out, grateful to Rosalie, who had taught him how to navigate in the curious world of the mind, flashing across water to the island of Hilo.

There *had* to be someone near the stand-by installation.

He searched; but there was no one. No one in the building. No one near the ruined field. No one in the village of the dead nearby. He was desperate; he became frantic; he was on the point of giving up, and then he found—someone? But it was a personality feebler than stricken Koitska's, a bare swampfire glow.

No matter. He entered it.

At once he screamed silently and left it again. He had never known such pain. A terrifying fire in the belly, a thunder past any migraine in the head, a thousand lesser aches and woes in every member. He could not imagine what person lived in such distress; but grimly he forced himself to enter again.

Moaning—it was astonishing how thick and animal-like the man's voice was—Chandler forced his borrowed body stumbling through the jungle. Time was growing very short. He drove it gasping at an awkward run across the airfield, dodged around one wrecked plane and blundered through the door.

The pain was intolerable. He was hardly able to maintain control; waves of nausea washed into his mind. How could he drive this agonizing hulk into the protracted, thoroughgoing job of total destruction?

Chandler stretched out the borrowed hand to pick up a heavy wrench even while he thought. But the hand would not grasp. He brought it to the weak, watering eyes.

The hand had no fingers. It ended in a ball of scar tissue. The other hand was nearly as misshapen.

Panicked, Chandler retreated from the body in a flash, back to his own; and then he began to think.

What sort of creature had he been inhabiting? Human? Why, yes, it must be human—the coronets gave no power over the bodies of animals. But it had not *felt* human. Chandler experienced one vertiginous moment when all possibilities seemed real, when visions of elves and beings from flying saucers danced in his brain; then sanity returned. Certainly it was human—someone sick, perhaps. Or insane. But human.

He could not understand that clawed club of a hand. But it didn't matter; he could use it, because he had used it. It was only a matter of figuring out how.

At that moment he heard a car race into the parking lot, spraying gravel. He looked out the window and saw Rosalie Pan's Porsche.

He unlocked the door for her and she came clattering

up the stairs as though chased by bears, glanced at Chandler, passed him by and dropped to her knees beside Koitska's body.

She looked up and said, "He's dead."

"I didn't kill him."

"I didn't say you did." She got up slowly, watching him. "You almost might as well be, love," she said. "I don't know what I can do for you now."

"No," agreed Chandler, nodding as though very frank and fair, "you can't help me much if he's dead." Full of guile he approached her, staring at Koitska's body. "But is he? I think I saw him breathe." Perplexed, she turned back to the body.

Chandler took a quick step, reached out and knocked the coronet off her head. It clung to her coiffure. Ruthlessly he grabbed it and yanked, and it came away with locks of her hair clinging to it.

She cried out and put a hand to her head, looking at him with astonishment and fear overriding the pain.

He said, breathing hard: "Maybe I can do something for myself."

Rosalie sobbed, "Love, you're crazy. You don't have a chance. Give it back to me, and— I'll try to help you, but— Love! Give it back, please!"

Chandler controlled his breathing and asked, very reasonably, "If you were me, would you give it back?"

"Yes! Please!" She took a step toward him, then stopped. Her pretty face was a grimace now, her hair torn and flying. She dropped her hands to her side and sobbed, "No, I wouldn't. But you must, love. Please. . . ."

Chandler said, "Sit down. Over there, next to his body. I want to think and I don't want you close to me." She started to object and he overrode her: "Sit down! Or—"

He touched the coronet on his own head.

She turned like a golem and sat down beside the obese old corpse. She sat watching him, her face passive and drained. Chandler tried to imagine for a moment what it must be like for her, in one second a member of that godlike society of superbeings who ruled the Earth, in another a mere mortal, a figure of clay whose body could be seized by him, Chandler or by any other of the Executive Committee. . . .

There was a threat in that. Chandler frowned. "I can't leave you there," he said, thinking out loud. "Your friend Fenell might drop in on you. Or somebody." Her expression did not change. He said briskly: "Get up. Get in that closet." When she hesitated, he added, "I'm not too good at controlling people. I might not be able to make you tie yourself up. But Rosalie, I could make you kill yourself."

The closet was small and uncomfortable, but it would hold her, and it had a lock. With Rosalie out of the way, Chandler paused for only a moment. There were details to think out. . . .

But he had a plan. He could strike a blow. He could end the menace of the Executive Committee forever!

The key to the whole thing was that crippled creature on Hilo. He knew now what it was, and wondered that he had not understood before.

A leper! One of the patients at Molokai—the doctor had told him some had got away. Through that leper, Chandler calculated, he could find a way to destroy the installation on Hilo—if nothing else offered, he could contrive to disable the generator, or break open its fuel storage supply and set fire to the building.

And the other installation was right here in this building, within his grasp! He could destroy them both, one through the leper, the other in his own person! And that's the end of the Executive Committee, he thought triumphantly, and then— And then—

He paused, suddenly downcast.

And then, of course, they would know something was wrong. There were a thousand of them. They would come here. They would kill him.

And they would rebuild the equipment that would give them back the world.

Chandler was close to weeping. So near to victory! And yet it was out of his reach. . . .

Except, he thought, that there was something about the standby installation that was different. What had Hsi said? A different frequency. And Koitska had had two coronets with him on the island. . . .

Chandler did not delay. Perhaps he was wrong. Perhaps it would not work. Perhaps his memory played him false, or his assumptions were in error, or Koitska had reset the frequency in the days since . . . perhaps anything, there were more unknown factors than he could guess at . . . but still there was a chance!

He leaped out of his body, poised himself to get his bearings and fled through the luminous gray mists toward Hilo. Steeling himself to the pain, he entered the body of the leper and loped shamblingly back toward the duplicate installation.

Five minutes later the generator coughed and spun, and the components came to life. Chandler had no way to test them, to determine what sort of signal they were generating; but he had helped put the installation together and, as far as he could see, it was operating perfectly.

He abandoned the body of the leper with gratitude, and stood up in his own.

Five minutes more and the master transmitter was stilled. Chandler had pulled the switch.

When he found Koitska's standby-frequency coronet and placed it on his head there was only one person in all the world who possessed the terrifying powers of a member of the Executive Committee, and that person was Chandler.

He stood there for a moment with his eyes closed, very tired and very calm. He knew what he had to do, but there was something, he felt, that he should do first. He waited, but could not remember what it was; and so a moment later he left his body and soared off in search of his first quarry.

It was not for some time that it came to him what he had wanted to do. He had wanted to pray.

It was all working; his best hopes were coming true! The installation on Hilo functioned perfectly and Chandler was, in fact, the master of the islands and thus of the world!

He accepted it without triumph. Perhaps the triumph would come later, but first he had work to do. For he had been wrong, he saw now, in thinking that the destruction of the machines would free the world from its tyranny. Koitska had not been the only scientist among the exec. Surely others knew the theory behind the electronic wizardry that gave them control; surely there were plans and wiring diagrams in some safe file, perhaps in a dozen of them, that could be brought out and used again. It was necessary to destroy the machinery, yes; but it was also necessary to destroy the plans ... not only the plans on paper but the plans that might linger in the brains of the members of the Exec.

It was, in fact, necessary to kill them all.

It was not only necessary, thought Chandler objectively, it was rather easy. It was child's play. All you had to do was the sort of thing members of the Exec had been doing for fun or in furtherance of a purpose every day for years. All you had to do was what he was doing. Up out of the body, and search for the queerly distorted sluggish sort of creature that turned out to be a human mind; enter it; and there you were in the body of a man or woman. You glanced in a mirror or touched the body's head with the body's hand—to check to see if it wore a coronet, of course. It if did, the body had to be destroyed. There were many ways of doing that. Simple household objects could be employed—a knife, a bottle of iodine to drink, sometimes you could find a gun.

Carefully and scientifically Chandler experimented with modes of suicide. He tried them all. He discovered that, failing all else, you really could choke yourself to death; but it was difficult and slow, and quite painful; he only did that once. He discovered that even a nail file, sawed vigorously enough across a throat, would ultimately open the artery that would spill out the life. He set fire to one house and trapped himself in a closet, but that was slow, too; drowned himself in a bathtub, but it took so irritatingly long for the tub to fill. Knives were almost always available if you just took the trouble to look, though; and saws, chisels, barbecue forks, scythes—almost anything with an edge could be used.

When Chandler had first learned that the "flame spirits" were human beings he had dreamed at night about them, and wakened to wonder how it must feel to kill oneself over and over again in some other flesh.

Now he knew. It felt very painful and very wearing; but of emotion—regret, sorrow, shame—there was little or none. It became very quickly a job. Like any other job, it was susceptible to time study and rationalization; after the first hour, when Chandler realized he had only managed seven deaths and would at that rate pass out from exhaustion before he had made himself safe against attack, he systematically improved his methods, finally settling for the quickest and easiest of them all. Too bad, he thought as he slew and slew, that it was only good in two-story buildings; annoying that the Hawaiians had gone in so heavily for ranch houses; but it was quite possible to kill yourself by leaping from a second-story window, provided only that you had the resolution to land headfirst. . . . The orgy of killing went on and on, all that day, and all that night, killing, killing in widening circles from the TWA Message Center, killing everything that wore a coronet and then as he grew wearier and more careless—and realized that the execs might by then have begun taking their useless coronets off, killing everything that moved.

He stopped only when he realized that he was in the fringes of Honolulu itself.

He had lost count long since, but he had surely killed a thousand times—and died a thousand times. No doubt some execs still survived, but he no longer had a way to distinguish them from the slaves. He stopped for that reason . . . and because he was tired beyond further effort . . . and most of all because blood had washed away his passions.

He was spent.

He slumped against a wall for a moment, back in his own body. And then he stood up, and took off the coronet and, dangling it from one hand, walked out into the dawn of a new world.

Chandler the giant killer looked upon his world and did not find it good.

Exhaustion diminished all his emotions, but he was aware that this was wrong. He should be exultant! He should be shouting with joy, caroling his gratitude to God; and he was not.

Why, he told himself reasonably, every most fantastic prayer of the past years had been granted at once! In one night he had avenged New York and the Orphalese, the incinerated millions of Russia and the raped slaves in Honolulu. . . .

But he could not help feeling that the job was not really done after all. He swung the coronet idly in his hand, staring blankly at the lightening sky, while a sly and treasonable voice in a corner of his mind whispered to him.

Who held this coronet held the world, said the voice in his mind.

He nodded, for that was true. Absently he poked at the steel-bright filigree of the thing, as a man might caress the pretty rug which once had been the skin of a tiger poised to kill him. It was such a small thing to hold so much power. . . .

Chandler went back into the building and brewed himself strong black coffee. He could hear Rosalie Pan stirring inside the closet where he had left her; in a minute he would let her out, he thought. Not just yet, but in a minute. As soon as he had thought things out. As soon as he had made up his mind to an extremely important decision. For it was true that the job was not quite done yet. The plans had to be located—and destroyed, of course. Naturally, destroyed. Survivors of the Exec had to be found, and also destroyed.

Yes, there was much to do. While he was waiting for the coffee to seep through its filter he slipped the coronet casually back atop his head. Only for a while, of course. A very little while. He pledged himself solemnly that there would definitely be no question about that. He would wear it just long enough to clean up all the loose ends—just that long and not one second longer, he pledged, and knew as he pledged it that he lied.

*Ballantine Books is proud to announce
publication of one of the great imaginative
works of our time*

THE AUTHORIZED EDITION
OF THE FAMOUS FANTASY TRILOGY

The Lord of the Rings

by J. R. R. Tolkien

**Newly revised and with a special
Foreword by the author**

Volume I
THE FELLOWSHIP OF THE RING

Volume II
THE TWO TOWERS

Volume III
THE RETURN OF THE KING

Note: This—and only this—is the Authorized Edition, published by arrangement with the author and his publisher, the Houghton Mifflin Company of Boston.

Published in three volumes, uniformly priced at 95¢

To order by mail, send $1.00 for each volume ($3.00 for the complete set) to Dept. C. S., Ballantine Books, 101 Fifth Ave., New York, N. Y. 10003. Please be sure to enclose full return address and Zip Code number.